ADULT LEARNER SERIES

Killer in a Trance?

JUDITH ANDREWS GREEN
DIRECTOR,
OXFORD HILLS ADULT AND
COMMUNITY EDUCATION
SCHOOL ADMINISTRATIVE DISTRICT #17
SOUTH PARIS, MAINE

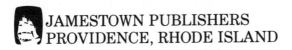

JAMESTOWN PUBLISHERS
PROVIDENCE, RHODE ISLAND

Catalog No. 208

Killer in a Trance?

Copyright © 1985 by
Judith Andrews Green

Cover and Story Illustrations by
Bob Giuliani

Printed in the United States AL

90 91 92 6 5 4 3

ISBN 0-89061-426-1

Titles in This Series

To
my best beloveds,
Sarah and Roger

To the Reader

Sue went to Lorenzo Lang, the hypnotist, to try to get rid of her headaches.

Everything seemed to be going fine, until the murder. Then she had to find out—*what had happened while she was in the trance?*

How could she find out? You'll have to read the story to learn the answer.

Before each chapter of the story, there are words for you to read and learn. The words are given in sentences, so that you can see how they will be used in the story. After each chapter, there are questions for you to answer. The questions will give you an idea of how well you are reading.

Also following each chapter is a section called Language Skills. It has lessons that will help you to read, write and spell better.

The last two parts of each unit deal with Life Skills. Life Skills are things you need to know about and know how to do to get along in life.

The answers to all the questions and exercises are in the back of the book. You can check your answers to see if they are right.

We hope you will like reading *Killer in a Trance?* and learning all the things this book teaches.

Contents

How to Use This Book

Study the words in the box. Then read the sentences below with your teacher. Look carefully at the words in boldface type.

cigarette	headaches	loading dock	straight
early	hypnotist	office	theater
eyes	hypnotize	questions	typewriter
forehead	laugh	relax	voice
forward	listen	storage	warehouse

1. These **headaches** were driving her crazy!
2. She put the cover on her **typewriter**.
3. Sue worked for Clark's Moving and **Storage**.
4. She put on her coat and stepped out of her **office**.
5. Out in the **warehouse**, everyone was getting ready to go home.
6. I didn't tell you that you could leave **early**.
7. The men on the **loading dock** put a few more things on the vans.
8. May Lee was smoking a **cigarette**.
9. Let's go to the **theater** tonight.
10. There's a show tonight. A **hypnotist**!
11. He's going to **hypnotize** people who come up on stage.
12. He put his hand on May Lee's **forehead**.
13. He began to talk in a quiet **voice**.
14. Put your hands in your lap. **Relax**. Just relax.
15. You are very sleepy. Your **eyes** are heavy.
16. Her head tipped **forward**, and her hair fell down around her face.
17. The crowd began to **laugh**.
18. They stood staring **straight** ahead, right where he had stopped them.
19. Now **listen** to me. Listen very carefully.
20. I'd like to ask you some **questions**.

18   KILLER IN A TRANCE?

1. Learn the Preview Words

Say the words in the box. Then read the sentences. Try to learn the words. See if you know what each sentence means.

Sue looked at the clock. It was almost five o'clock at last.

She looked down at the pile of papers on her desk, put her hands over her face, and groaned. Her head hurt—it had been hurting all day. These headaches were driving her crazy!

She took her hands away from her face. "Come on," she told herself, "it's Friday! Time to go home!" She piled up the papers on her desk and put the cover on her typewriter. No more typing until Monday.

Sue had been working for Clark's Moving and Storage for three years, typing up the work orders that told the drivers where to go. It wasn't a bad job, but she felt so tired all the time. And that Mr. Clark . . .

Slowly Sue stood up, put on her coat, and stepped out of her little office. Out in the warehouse, everyone was getting ready to go home. The men were closing up the trucks. People from the main office were putting on their coats. Everyone was moving quickly, all talking at once. It was Friday! They had places to go and things to do. Some of them were already going out the door, calling back, "Good-bye! Have a nice weekend!"

Suddenly the door of the main office flew open and Mr. Clark burst into the warehouse. His face was red and his eyes were bugging out of his head. His eyes were a light blue, almost like water, but the rims of his eyes were red. "What do you people think you're doing?" he shouted. He stood in the middle of the warehouse and looked angrily around him. "Where do you think you're going? It's not five o'clock yet!"

No one moved. No one said a word. Everyone just stood where they were and looked at him. The clock on the wall showed one minute before five.

THE HYPNOTIST   19

2. Read the Chapter

As you read, try to follow the events of the story. See if you can figure out how the killer will be caught in the end.

Directions. Answer these questions about the chapter you have just read. Put an *x* in the box beside the best answer to each question.

1. (A) Suddenly the door of the main office flew open and Mr. Clark burst into the warehouse. That means that he
   - ☐ a. broke the door to the warehouse.
   - ☐ b. broke the door to the warehouse.
   - ☐ c. went in slowly and quietly.
   - ☐ d. broke in when the warehouse was closed for the night.

2. (D) You can tell that Clark
   - ☐ a. was a good boss.
   - ☐ b. shouted at his workers all the time.
   - ☐ c. wanted to go home early.
   - ☐ d. knew the best way to run a warehouse.

3. (B) Why couldn't Sue go to visit her father?
   - ☐ a. He lived too far away.
   - ☐ b. Clark didn't like him.
   - ☐ c. She couldn't get any time off from work.
   - ☐ d. She thought that he didn't want to see her.

3. Answer: Comprehension Questions

Put an *x* in the box next to the best answer to each question. Read all ten questions first and answer the easy ones. Then go back and answer the hard ones.

4. Correct Your Answers

Use the Answer Key on page 212. Circle any answers you got wrong, and mark the right answers with an *x*.

5. Fill in the Graphs

Fill in the graph on page 221 to show your comprehension score. Use the graph on page 223 to chart your skills.

6. Read: Language Skills

This comes after the questions. Read the pages and do the exercises. Use the Answer Key that begins on page 213 to correct the exercises.

Language Skills/Chapter 1

Roots and Suffixes

Look at the pairs of words below.

hope   hopeful
good   goodness
thank   thankless

You can see that the second word in each pair is made from the first word. In the first example, the word *hopeful* is made from the word *hope. Hope* is called a *root.* That root + the ending *-ful* makes the new word *hopeful.* An ending that changes the meaning of a word is called a *suffix.* In the second example, *goodness* is made from the word *good.* The root *good* + the suffix *-ness* gives us the new word *goodness.* In the third example, the new word *thankless* is made from the root *thank* + the suffix *-less.*

You can see that in the examples above it was easy to make the new words. We just added a suffix to a root. But sometimes slight spelling changes must be made when adding a suffix to a root. Look at the pairs of words below.

write   writing
stop   stopped
beauty   beautiful

In these word pairs, the second word is made from the first word. In the first pair, *writing* is made from the root *write* + the suffix *-ing.* But the new word is *writing,* not *writeing.* The *e* was dropped from *write* before adding the *-ing.* In the second pair, *stopped* is made from the root *stop* + the suffix *-ed.* But the new word is *stopped,*

34   KILLER IN A TRANCE?

7. Read: Understanding Life Skills
Read these pages and follow the step-by-step lessons.

. Paychecks and Stubs
People who have jobs are usually paid once a week or once every two weeks. They are given their earnings in the form of a *paycheck*. A paycheck does not give a worker all the money that he or she has earned, however. A part of the earnings is taken by the government for *income tax*. Another part is taken for *Social Security taxes*, or *FICA*. Workers also sometimes allow their employers to take out money for such things as insurance, retirement plans, or union dues. All the amounts subtracted from a worker's earnings for such purposes are called *deductions*. In this lesson we will talk about only the government deductions that are taken from the earnings of all workers.

With every paycheck, a worker gets a check stub. The stub is a report of the worker's earnings and deductions. A stub shows:

1. how much money the worker earned for the pay period
2. how much money was taken, or deducted, for taxes from the total earnings

A sample paycheck and stub are shown below.

---

8. Practice: Applying Life Skills
Read the instructions and do the Life Skills exercises. Take your time. Do the work carefully. Try to remember what you just read about understanding life skills. Use the Answer Key that begins on page 216 to correct the exercises.

Reading Paychecks and Stubs
You know that a worker does not take home all the money he or she earns on the job. The employer deducts part of the worker's earnings to pay the worker's federal and state income taxes and Social Security taxes. Workers are paid with paychecks. A paycheck comes with a stub. A stub is a record of:

1. the worker's gross earnings
2. all deductions taken from the worker's earnings
3. the worker's net, or take-home, pay

Exercise 1
A paycheck stub gives information about a worker's earnings and about deductions from those earnings. The boxes on the stub are labeled to give the worker clear and complete information about his or her earnings.

For each question below, pick out the label that would mark the box on a paycheck stub that would show the information asked for. Circle the correct label. Then copy it on the line provided. The first one has been done for you as an example.

1. What are the worker's total earnings? That amount would be found in the box marked

WITHHOLDING TAX   NET EARNINGS   (GROSS EARNINGS)

Gross Earnings

---

9. Read the Chapter Again
Go back to the story and read it once more. This time, as you read, try to feel all the interest and excitement the writer has built in.

Then, go on to the Preview Words for the next chapter.

Sue looked at the clock. It was almost five o'clock at last.

She looked down at the pile of papers on her desk, put her hands over her face, and groaned. Her head hurt—it had been hurting all day. These headaches were driving her crazy!

She took her hands away from her face. "Come on," she told herself, "it's Friday! Time to go home!" She piled up the papers on her desk and put the cover on her typewriter. No more typing until Monday.

Sue had been working for Clark's Moving and Storage for three years, typing up the work orders that told the drivers where to go. It wasn't a bad job, but she felt so tired all the time. And that Mr. Clark . . .

Slowly Sue stood up, put on her coat, and stepped out of her little office. Out in the warehouse, everyone was getting ready to go home. The men were closing up the trucks. People from the main office were putting on their coats. Everyone was moving quickly, all talking at once. It was Friday! They had places to go and things to do. Some of them were already going out the door, calling back, "Good-bye! Have a nice weekend!"

Suddenly the door of the main office flew open and Mr. Clark burst into the warehouse. His face was red and his eyes were bugging out of his head. His eyes were a light blue, almost like water, but the rims of his eyes were red. "What do you people think you're doing?" he shouted. He stood in the middle of the warehouse and looked angrily around him. "Where do you think you're going? It's not five o'clock yet!"

No one moved. No one said a word. Everyone just stood where they were and looked at him. The clock on the wall showed one minute before five.

1

The Hypnotist

Study the words in the box. Then read the sentences below with your teacher. Look carefully at the words in boldface type.

cigarette	headaches	loading dock	straight
early	hypnotist	office	theater
eyes	hypnotize	questions	typewriter
forehead	laugh	relax	voice
forward	listen	storage	warehouse

1. These **headaches** were driving her crazy!
2. She put the cover on her **typewriter**.
3. Sue worked for Clark's Moving and **Storage**.
4. She put on her coat and stepped out of her **office**.
5. Out in the **warehouse**, everyone was getting ready to go home.
6. I didn't tell you that you could leave **early**.
7. The men on the **loading dock** put a few more things on the vans.
8. May Lee was smoking a **cigarette**.
9. Let's go to the **theater** tonight.
10. There's a show tonight. A **hypnotist**!
11. He's going to **hypnotize** people who come up on stage.
12. He put his hand on May Lee's **forehead**.
13. He began to talk in a quiet **voice**.
14. Put your hands in your lap. **Relax**. Just relax.
15. You are very sleepy. Your **eyes** are heavy.
16. Her head tipped **forward**, and her hair fell down around her face.
17. The crowd began to **laugh**.
18. They stood staring **straight** ahead, right where he had stopped them.
19. Now **listen** to me. Listen very carefully.
20. I'd like to ask you some **questions**.

Sue looked at the clock. It was almost five o'clock at last.

She looked down at the pile of papers on her desk, put her hands over her face, and groaned. Her head hurt—it had been hurting all day. These headaches were driving her crazy!

She took her hands away from her face. "Come on," she told herself, "it's Friday! Time to go home!" She piled up the papers on her desk and put the cover on her typewriter. No more typing until Monday.

Sue had been working for Clark's Moving and Storage for three years, typing up the work orders that told the drivers where to go. It wasn't a bad job, but she felt so tired all the time. And that Mr. Clark . . .

Slowly Sue stood up, put on her coat, and stepped out of her little office. Out in the warehouse, everyone was getting ready to go home. The men were closing up the trucks. People from the main office were putting on their coats. Everyone was moving quickly, all talking at once. It was Friday! They had places to go and things to do. Some of them were already going out the door, calling back, "Good-bye! Have a nice weekend!"

Suddenly the door of the main office flew open and Mr. Clark burst into the warehouse. His face was red and his eyes were bugging out of his head. His eyes were a light blue, almost like water, but the rims of his eyes were red. "What do you people think you're doing?" he shouted. He stood in the middle of the warehouse and looked angrily around him. "Where do you think you're going? It's not five o'clock yet!"

No one moved. No one said a word. Everyone just stood where they were and looked at him. The clock on the wall showed one minute before five.

"I didn't tell you that you could leave early!" Clark shouted. "Now get back to work! You men on the loading dock, you have time to put a few more things on those vans! You over there, get back into that office! And don't think you're going to put in for any overtime pay! You've been wasting my time!"

People began to move toward the vans or the main office. Sue went back into her office and closed the door. That Mr. Clark . . . She sat down and put her hands over her face again. Her headache was worse.

She tried to think happy thoughts about the weekend. What should she do with herself? She wished that she could go to see her father. She hadn't seen him in a long time, and she missed him. But no, she couldn't do that. She always felt as if he and her stepmother didn't want her around.

Sue sat and waited until ten after five. Then she

stuck her head out the door and looked all around the warehouse. Everything was quiet. Quietly, one by one, people were going out the door.

Sue looked at the door of the main office to make sure that it was closed. Then she stepped out of her little office and closed the door. She hurried to the big warehouse door and stepped outside. Another week was over.

Her friend May Lee was waiting for her on the sidewalk, smoking a cigarette. There were two or three cigarette butts on the sidewalk around her feet. When May Lee saw Sue, she pushed back her long black hair and smiled. "What took you so long?" she asked. "I was getting worried! I thought maybe the old man had eaten you!" She took another drag on her cigarette. "I had just gone out the door when I heard Clark yelling. I didn't dare go back in."

"You didn't miss anything," Sue said. "Just his 'You're Wasting My Time' bit."

"Oh well, we're out of his way until Monday," May Lee said. "What should we do tonight? I know, let's go to the theater! There's a show tonight, a hypnotist! He's going to hypnotize people—anyone who wants to go up on stage. Let's go see him!"

"Oh, I don't know," Sue said. "It does sound like fun. But I have a headache, so I think I'll just go home."

"You and your headaches! There must be something you can take for them. Have you been to a doctor?"

"Yes, I've tried three doctors, but there isn't anything they can do for me."

"So forget your worries!" May Lee said as she threw her cigarette down and stepped on it. "You're coming with me, and we're going to see that hypnotist! I'm not going to let you miss out on everything." She grabbed Sue's arm and pulled her down the street.

As they walked along, talking, Sue began to feel better. It was good to be outside. Suddenly May Lee grabbed Sue's arm again and gasped, "Oh, no!"

A man was coming down the sidewalk toward them, walking a little dog on a long leash. "Keep it away from me!" May Lee said quickly, pulling Sue in front of her.

The man and the little dog went by the two women. Then the dog turned suddenly and ran up to Sue and May Lee, wagging its tail. "No! No! Don't let it jump up on me!" May Lee said. She kept Sue between herself and the dog.

"There's nothing to be afraid of. See, it's friendly," Sue said, bending down and patting the little dog. The man smiled at Sue and called to the dog.

"Oh!" May Lee gasped as she watched the man and the dog go off down the sidewalk. Her hands shook as she lit another cigarette. "I *hate* dogs!"

"But it was just a *little* dog," Sue said. "It wouldn't hurt you."

"I don't care. I hate all dogs. I'll take Mr. Clark over a dog any day.

Sue laughed. "That bad?" she asked.

"That bad." May Lee pushed her hair back and took a deep breath. "Come on, let's go get something to eat before the show."

There was a big crowd at the theater. When the hypnotist, a tall thin man with black hair, came out on stage, the crowd clapped loudly. The man bowed, then put his hand up for quiet.

"I am Lorenzo Lang, the hypnotist," he said. "I am known all over the world. But now, I have moved to your city. This is my first show in my new home."

"Isn't he great?" May Lee said in Sue's ear. "He's going to call for people to go up and be hypnotized. Let's go up, OK?"

"Oh, no," Sue said, "I could never do anything like that!"

"Well *I'm* going to!" May Lee said.

When Lang asked, "Who will come up to be hypnotized?", May Lee put her hand up quickly. Lots of other people put their hands up too, waving so that Lang would see them. Lang pointed to some of them, saying, "You and you, and you, and you." He pointed at May Lee. "You there, with the brown coat." May Lee jumped up and made her way to the stage with the others.

Now there were ten people on the stage with Lang. He told them to sit down in the row of chairs behind him. "I will now put you to sleep," he told them. "There is no danger. It will not hurt you. Just relax. Put your feet flat on the floor in front of you, put your hands in your lap, and relax. Just relax."

He went to the first chair, where May Lee was sitting, and put his hand on May Lee's forehead. For a moment he just looked at her. Sue watched him, holding her breath.

Then he began to talk in a quiet voice. "Relax. You are very relaxed. You are getting sleepy. You are very sleepy—very, very sleepy. Your eyes are heavy—so heavy that you can't hold them open any more." Sue saw May Lee's eyes fall shut. Her head tipped forward, and her long hair fell down around her face. "You are asleep," Lang went on. "You are in a deep sleep. You can't open your eyes. You are in a deep sleep."

As Lang stepped back, everyone stared at May Lee. She sat on the stage with her eyes shut. She did not move.

"Can you hear me?" Lang asked. "If you can hear me, nod your head." Slowly, slowly, May Lee nodded her head once.

"Stand up," Lang told her. Slowly, May Lee stood up. "Walk to the front of the stage." May Lee walked forward, her eyes shut tight. "Stop," Lang said, when she got to the front of the stage. He took her arm and held it out in front of her, saying, "Your arm is very stiff. You can't bend it. You must keep it right where it is." Then he walked away. May Lee stood there just as he had left her.

Lang went up to the man in the second chair and quickly put him to sleep. Then he pushed on the man's forehead until the man's head was tipped back. He left him like that and went on to the third person.

Sue didn't watch him—she couldn't take her eyes off May Lee. May Lee just stood there at the front of the stage with her arm held out stiffly in front of her. "How can she do that?" Sue asked herself. "Her arm must be so tired."

Now five of the people on the stage were hypnotized, sitting with their eyes shut tight. Some of them had their heads tipped back. They did not move.

Lang told a man to stand up. He led the man to the front of the stage and said, "Open your eyes. Can you see me?"

"Yes," the man said in a flat, strange voice.

"Now I want you to walk up these stairs," Lang said, pointing at the bare stage. "The stairs are very steep. Do you see them?"

"Yes, I see them," the man said.

"Good. Now walk up the stairs. Don't forget to lift your feet high so that you won't fall. Go."

The man began to move his feet. He lifted one foot high, and then put it back down in the same place. Then he lifted the other foot, then the first foot again. He didn't move forward, but he looked as if he were going up stairs. The crowd began to laugh.

"It's hard work, isn't it?" Lang asked the man. "The stairs are very long, and you're getting tired. You'd better hold on to the railing."

The man began to look tired. He reached out his hands and pulled himself up, step by step, holding on to thin air, until he was gasping for breath. Yet he never moved forward.

"All right," Lang said, "you're at the top. Be careful—don't fall!" The man looked down, as if he were looking down a long way. He gasped and grabbed for the railing of thin air.

"All right," Lang said, putting his hand on the man's forehead, "you are back down on the stage again. Sleep." The man's hands dropped to his sides, and his head tipped back. He did not move.

Now Lang turned to another man. "You're a dog," he told the man. "Speak, boy!" The man began to bark like a dog.

"Good boy," Lang said as he patted the man's head. Then he turned to the man sitting next to him. "You're a cat. You feel good. Show me what cats do when they feel good." The man got up and rubbed against him, purring like a cat.

"Watch out! Here comes a dog!" Lang said. He turned to the man who thought he was a dog. "Look, a cat! Get that cat!" While the dog-man barked and chased the cat-man around the stage, the crowd laughed and laughed.

Sue just sat and stared. Two men were running around the stage. They didn't know who they were. They didn't even know where they were. Yet they never fell off the stage or bumped into May Lee. May Lee was still standing at the front of the stage with her arm held out in front of her. She never looked at the men running around her. She never moved.

Lang stopped the dog and cat by telling them, "Sleep." They stood staring straight ahead, right where he had stopped them.

The hypnotist went on with the show. He gave one woman a coin, then told her that it was hot. The crowd laughed as she quickly dropped the coin and rubbed her hand. He told another woman to stand very stiff, then he laid her down between two chairs, with her head on one chair and her feet on the other. She didn't bend in the middle at all.

The hypnotist made the people do one thing after another, while the crowd cheered and cheered. Then, one by one, he woke all the people up and sent them back to their seats. May Lee was all alone with him on the stage now. What was he going to make her do?

Lang stood next to May Lee and talked to the crowd. "I have shown you what people will do when they are hypnotized," he said. "A hypnotist has made you gasp. A hypnotist has made you laugh. But now I will show you the good that a hypnotist can do." He turned to May Lee. "You are afraid of something, aren't you? What are you afraid of?"

May Lee talked for the first time. "Dogs," she said in a strange, low voice.

"Did something happen to make you afraid of dogs?"

"Yes."

"Is it all right for me and the other people to know what happened?" Lang asked.

"Yes."

Sue sat forward in her seat so as to hear every word. May Lee sure *was* afraid of dogs!

"Were you scared by a dog at one time?" Lang asked.

"Yes," May Lee said.

"How old were you?"

"I was two years old," May Lee said. The crowd gasped. No one could remember back that far!

"Now you are two years old," Lang told May Lee. "A dog is coming toward you. It is very near you. Tell me what is happening."

Suddenly May Lee began to cry. "Doggie coming!"

she cried in a little girl's voice. "Brother, take doggie away!"

"What does the doggie look like?" Lang asked softly.

"Doggie brown! He jump on me! He jump on May Lee!" She put her arms up in front of her face.

"How big is the doggie?" Lang asked.

"Big! This big!" May Lee said, holding her arms wide. She was crying harder now.

"This big?" Lang asked, holding out his arms to show a much smaller dog.

"Yes! Oh, take him away! He jump on me!" The two-year-old May Lee was crying.

"Now listen to me," Lang said, "listen very carefully. I am holding the doggie in my arms. Do you see him?" May Lee nodded her head, sniffing. "All right. Now you are going to grow. You are growing up. You are six years old. Now look at the dog I have in my arms. He doesn't look quite so big now, does he?" Lang asked.

"No, he doesn't."

"Now you are growing again. You are ten years old. Look at the dog I have in my arms. He's not very big at all, is he?"

"No," May Lee said. "He's just a puppy."

"Now you are growing again. You are growing up. You are now a woman, back to your real age. Now look at this little puppy I have in my arms. This is your brother's puppy. Look at its soft brown fur. Isn't it cute?"

"Yes, it's a cute little thing," May Lee said. Sue gasped when she heard that. She had never heard May Lee say anything nice about a dog—even a cute little puppy. What was happening?

"Now I'm going to put your brother's puppy down." Lang bent down as if he were putting something down on the stage. "The puppy is running over to you. Can you pat him?" May Lee bent down and patted the air. "Now he's jumping up on you," Lang went on. "Puppies do that. They like to play. Do you see him jumping up on you?" May Lee nodded. "Tell him to get down."

"Down, boy," May Lee said. "Down, Brownie."

"He got down," Lang said. "A puppy could scare a little girl by jumping up on her. The puppy would seem very big to a little girl. But not to a grown woman. A grown woman would know he was just a puppy. A grown woman would tell him to get down. Isn't that right?"

"Yes."

"You won't be afraid of dogs any more. You will be careful with strange dogs, of course, but you will not be afraid of all dogs. You will feel like any other grown woman."

"Yes," May Lee said.

Lang turned to face the crowd. "This will go on even after this woman wakes up. If there is anyone in the crowd who knows her, you will see a change in her. She will not be afraid of dogs any more." He turned back to May Lee and said, "When I count to five, you will wake up—one . . . two . . . three . . . four . . . five!"

May Lee blinked, and a change came over her face. She didn't look strange any more. She looked like herself again. She was awake.

"I'd like to ask you some questions," Lang said.

"Sure, go ahead!" May Lee said, smiling and pushing her long hair back from her face.

"How long have you been up here on the stage?" Lang asked.

"I've been up here just a minute or two. A minute ago I was sitting in that chair over there," May Lee said, pointing to the back of the stage. "I don't remember standing up."

"Did you hear or see anything?" Lang asked.

"No, I must have been asleep," May Lee said. The crowd laughed.

"One more question," Lang said. "Were you afraid of dogs?"

"Yes, I was. How did you know that?"

Lang just smiled. "Why were you afraid of dogs?"

"I don't know," May Lee said. "I just always was, as far back as I can remember."

"How do you feel about dogs now?" Lang asked.

"Why, I . . . I don't think I'm afraid of them any more!" May Lee said. "I used to be afraid to *think* about them! But not now. I'm not afraid of them anymore!"

The crowd clapped as May Lee left the stage. They clapped and cheered loudly as Lang bowed again and again. They went on clapping even after the hypnotist had left the stage.

Sue clapped and cheered loudest of all.

Directions. Answer these questions about the chapter you have just read. Put an *x* in the box beside the best answer to each question.

1. (A) Suddenly the door of the main office flew open and Mr. Clark *burst* into the warehouse. That means that he

    □ a. went in very quickly and suddenly.
    □ b. broke the door to the warehouse.
    □ c. went in slowly and quietly.
    □ d. broke in when the warehouse was closed for the night.

2. (D) You can tell that Clark

    □ a. was a good boss.
    □ b. shouted at his workers all the time.
    □ c. wanted to go home early.
    □ d. knew the best way to run a warehouse.

3. (B) Why couldn't Sue go to visit her father?

    □ a. He lived too far away.
    □ b. Clark didn't like him.
    □ c. She couldn't get any time off from work.
    □ d. She thought that he didn't want to see her.

4. (B) Why did Sue have to go to three doctors?

☐ a. She smoked too many cigarettes.
☐ b. She got very bad headaches.
☐ c. A dog bit her.
☐ d. She often fell asleep at her desk.

5. (E) How did May Lee feel about dogs at the beginning of the story?

☐ a. She liked little dogs, but not big ones.
☐ b. She liked all dogs.
☐ c. She was afraid of all dogs.
☐ d. She liked dogs as long as they were tied up.

6. (C) Which of these things did Lang do first?

☐ a. He made a woman lie down across two chairs.
☐ b. He gave a woman a coin and told her that it was hot.
☐ c. He made a man think he was climbing up some stairs.
☐ d. He made May Lee stand with her arm held out.

7. (A) The hypnotized man reached out his hands and pulled himself up, holding on to *thin air*. This means that

☐ a. the air was so thin that he could not breathe.
☐ b. the man's hands were very thin.
☐ c. he was holding on to nothing.
☐ d. the man was trying to hold on to a very thin railing.

8. (E) Why did Lang tell the two men that they were a cat and a dog?

    ☐ a. He wanted to help them get over their fear of dogs.

    ☐ b. He wanted to put on a fun show for the crowd.

    ☐ c. He wanted to make them hurt each other.

    ☐ d. He wanted to see if they would fall off the stage.

9. (C) Which of these things happened last?

    ☐ a. Lang made May Lee think she was two years old.

    ☐ b. Lang asked May Lee what she was afraid of.

    ☐ c. Lang asked May Lee how she felt about dogs now.

    ☐ d. Lang told May Lee to wake up.

10. (D) Why did May Lee say that she had been on the stage for only a minute or two?

    ☐ a. She had been hypnotized, so she didn't remember anything that had happened.

    ☐ b. While she was hypnotized, Lang told her to say that.

    ☐ c. She went up on the stage only at the end of the show.

    ☐ d. She wanted to make the crowd laugh.

Skills Used to Answer Questions

A. Recognizing Words in Context   B. Recalling Facts

C. Keeping Events in Order   D. Making Inferences

E. Understanding Main Ideas

Roots and Suffixes

Look at the pairs of words below.

hope   hopeful

good   goodness

thank   thankless

You can see that the second word in each pair is made from the first word. In the first example, the word *hopeful* is made from the word *hope*. *Hope* is called a *root*. That root + the ending *-ful* makes the new word *hopeful*. An ending that changes the meaning of a word is called a *suffix*. In the second example, *goodness* is made from the word *good*. The root *good* + the suffix *-ness* gives us the new word *goodness*. In the third example, the new word *thankless* is made from the root *thank* + the suffix *-less*.

You can see that in the examples above it was easy to make the new words. We just added a suffix to a root. But sometimes slight spelling changes must be made when adding a suffix to a root. Look at the pairs of words below.

write   writing

stop   stopped

beauty   beautiful

In these word pairs, the second word is made from the first word. In the first pair, *writing* is made from the root *write* + the suffix *-ing*. But the new word is *writing*, not *writeing*. The *e* was dropped from *write* before adding the *-ing*. In the second pair, *stopped* is made from the root *stop* + the suffix *-ed*. But the new word is *stopped*, not *stoped*. The *p* at the end of *stop* was doubled. In the third pair, *beautiful* is made from the root *beauty* + the suffix *-ful*. But the new word is *beautiful*, not *beautyful*. The *y* at the end of *beauty* was changed to *i*.

Sometimes there is a spelling change when you make new words from roots and suffixes. Sometimes there is no spelling change. In the following chapters, you will learn some spelling rules. The rules will tell you:

1. when you need a spelling change to make a new word
2. how to make the spelling change you need

Exercise 1

Below is a list of roots and suffixes. You can make new words from these roots and suffixes. Just add the suffix to the root. No spelling changes are needed. Print the new words on the lines provided. The first one has been done for you as an example.

1. try + -ing   trying _____
2. fair + -ness _____
3. pave + -ment _____
4. open + -ing _____
5. park + -ed _____
6. cup + -ful _____
7. fit + -ness _____
8. act + -or _____

Exercise 2

A list of roots and suffixes and the new words made by putting them together is given below. Sometimes there is a spelling change in the new word, sometimes there is not. If there is a change in the new word, print *Spelling Change* on the line provided. If there is no spelling change, write *No Spelling Change* on the line. The first two have been done for you as examples.

1. end + -ing = ending __No Spelling Change__

2. love + -able = lovable __Spelling Change__

3. shop + -ing = shopping _____

4. arrive + -al = arrival _____

5. meet + -ing = meeting _____

6. teach + -er = teacher _____

7. happy + -ness = happiness _____

8. joy + -ous = joyous _____

9. merry + -ly = merrily _____

10. wonder + -ful = wonderful _____

Paychecks and Stubs

People who have jobs are usually paid once a week or once every two weeks. They are given their earnings in the form of a *paycheck.* A paycheck does not give a worker all the money that he or she has earned, however. A part of the earnings is taken by the government for *income tax.* Another part is taken for *Social Security taxes,* which is also called *FICA.* Workers also sometimes allow their employers to take out money for such things as insurance, retirement plans, or union dues. All the amounts subtracted from a worker's earnings for such purposes are called *deductions.* In this lesson we will talk about only the government deductions that are taken from the earnings of all workers.

With every paycheck, a worker gets a check *stub.* The stub is a report of the worker's earnings and deductions. A stub shows:

1. how much money the worker earned for the pay period
2. how much money was taken, or deducted, for taxes from the total earnings

A sample paycheck and stub are shown on the next page.

```
MATTAPOISETT DRY CLEANERS                                    4814
14 CANAL STREET                          DATE   Aug. 30  1985
MATTAPOISETT, MA 02809


PAY TO THE ORDER OF   SUSAN  BROWN
THREE  HUNDRED  SEVENTY-FIVE  and  83/100  $375.83


BAY BANK
BOSTON, MA                              Ethel Herman

1:  012345678 1:  011  043  011:         ETHEL HERMAN, TREASURER
```

PAYCHECK

STATEMENT OF EARNINGS   CHECK NO.
AND DEDUCTIONS   4814

MATTAPOISETT DRY CLEANERS

EMPLOYEE NAME	PAY PERIOD	DATE
SUSAN BROWN	8/16/85 – 8/30/85	9/5/85

| GROSS EARNINGS | WITHOLDING TAX | | F.I.C.A. | NET EARNINGS |
	FEDERAL	STATE		
469.81	53.07	10.10	30.81	375.83

PAYCHECK STUB

You can see from the paycheck that Susan Brown has
been given $375.83 for the pay period. The stub tells you
how much Susan Brown earned in all. It also tells how
much was deducted by her employer for state and federal
taxes.

Look at the check stub.

1. In the box marked "Date," you see the month, day and year that the paycheck was issued.
2. In the box marked "Pay Period," you are told that this check is payment to Susan Brown for work done from August 16, 1985 to August 30, 1985.
3. The box marked "Gross Earnings" tells how much Susan Brown earned during the pay period. *Gross* means the total income a worker earned—before deductions.
4. The box marked "Withholding Tax" tells how much was withheld for income taxes. Susan Brown has paid $53.07 in federal taxes. She has paid $10.10 in state taxes.
5. The box marked FICA tells how much of Susan Brown's pay was deducted for the payment of Social Security taxes. That amount is $30.81.
6. The box marked "Net Earnings" tells how much of Susan Brown's earnings are left after all deductions. Her new pay is the amount she gets in her paycheck. Net pay is also called *take-home pay*. It is the amount the worker actually takes home from the job.

Susan Brown will cash her paycheck. She will keep the stub. It is her record of what she has earned and of the deductions that have been taken from her earnings.

Reading Paychecks and Stubs

You know that a worker does not take home all the money he or she earns on the job. The employer deducts part of the worker's earnings to pay the worker's federal and state income taxes and Social Security (FICA) taxes. Workers are paid with paychecks. A paycheck comes with a stub. A stub is a record of:

1. the worker's gross earnings
2. all deductions taken from the worker's earnings
3. the worker's net, or take-home, pay

Exercise 1

A paycheck stub gives information about a worker's earnings and about deductions from those earnings. The boxes on the stub are labeled to give the worker clear and complete information about his or her earnings.

For each question below, pick out the label that would mark the box on a paycheck stub that would show the information asked for. Circle the correct label. Then copy it on the line provided. The first one has been done for you as an example.

1. What are the worker's total earnings? That amount would be found in the box marked

WITHHOLDING TAX   NET EARNINGS   (GROSS EARNINGS)

<u>Gross Earnings</u>

2. How much has been taken out for federal income tax? That amount would be found in the box marked

WITHHOLDING TAX FEDERAL   WITHHOLDING TAX STATE   FICA

___

3. When did the worker earn the money paid in this check? That information would be found in the box marked

PAY PERIOD   DATE   NET EARNINGS

___

4. When was this paycheck issued? That information would be found in the box marked

PAY PERIOD   DATE   NET EARNINGS

___

5. How much was withheld for the payment of Social Security (FICA) taxes? That amount would be found in the box marked

WITHHOLDING TAX FEDERAL   GROSS EARNINGS   FICA

___

6. How much is the worker's take-home pay? That amount would be found in the box marked

GROSS EARNINGS   NET PAY   PAY PERIOD

___

Exercise 2

Look on the paycheck and stub shown below to find the information needed to answer the questions that follow. The questions are about the worker's earnings and deductions. Print your answers in the spaces provided.

Hempstead Bus Corporation   **6540**
1300 Pike Road
Hempstead, Kentucky

                                            September 29, 1985

Pay to the Order of: ___*Leonard Parker*___

Four hundred sixty-five and $\frac{00}{100}$ | $465.00 |

Pioneer Banks
Hempstead, Ky.

1: 069148864: **022** 043 **011**

                                            Susan Dix, Treasurer

---

STATEMENT OF EARNINGS   Check No.
AND DEDUCTIONS   6540

HEMPSTEAD BUS CORPORATION

EMPLOYEE NAME	PAY PERIOD	DATE
Leonard Parker	4/15/85-4/26/85	4/29/85

GROSS EARNINGS	WITHOLDING TAX		F.I.C.A.	NET EARNINGS
	FEDERAL	STATE		
581.15	72.08	11.03	33.04	465.00

1. When Leonard Parker cashes his check, how much money will he get?

   _____

2. How much are Leonard Parker's total earnings for two weeks?

   _____

3. How much of Leonard Parker's earnings will go to the federal government for income tax?

   _____

4. How much will go to the federal government for Social Security?

   _____

5. How much of Leonard Parker's pay will go to the state government for taxes?

   _____

6. What is Leonard Parker's take-home pay?

   _____

2

Into a Trance

Study the words in the box. Then read the sentences below with your teacher. Look carefully at the words in boldface type.

answer	causing	foreman's	mumbled
apartment	company	hopefully	pocketbook
appointment	curtains	hour	scratching
because	downstairs	idea	wondered
building	elevator	ladies	write

1. They hurried back to May Lee's **apartment**.
2. They waited for her mother to **answer** the phone.
3. They had to get rid of the dog **because** it kept jumping up on me.
4. She ran out the front door of the **building**.
5. The man looked after them, **scratching** his head.
6. I just had a great **idea**!
7. So many things could be **causing** the headaches.
8. She works for Clark's Moving and Storage **Company**.
9. "Good morning, **ladies**!" a man's voice boomed.
10. She **wondered** if May Lee's cigarette had gone out.
11. I got you an **appointment** with him.
12. They got into the **elevator**.
13. I'll **write** you a check.
14. I work in the **foreman's** office, in the big warehouse.
15. "I know, I know," Lang **mumbled**.
16. The windows were covered with heavy **curtains**.
17. Maybe you could wait **downstairs**.
18. You will take your **pocketbook**, but you will leave your checkbook.
19. You will go into the office and stay there for one **hour**.
20. "Did you find out why I get headaches?" Sue asked **hopefully**.

That night, as Sue and May Lee made their way home from the theater, Sue told May Lee all about the hypnotist's show. She told her about all the things that Lang had made people do. "And you know what? You missed the whole thing!" Sue told her. "You slept through all of it!"

"It must have been really something!" May Lee said. "But what did he do about dogs? I've *always* been afraid of dogs, and now—I don't know—I just feel different."

"He made you think you were two years old," Sue said. "You sounded just like a little girl, and you were talking about your brother and his dog Brownie."

"I do have a brother," May Lee said. "He's three years older than I am. But I don't think he ever had a dog. No one in the family has ever talked about one."

"Well, maybe it was all a trick," Sue said. "Maybe Lang just made you say all those things."

"Let's call my mother!" May Lee said. "She would know if my brother ever had a dog."

As soon as they got back to May Lee's apartment, May Lee grabbed the phone. While she waited for her mother to answer, she pulled out a cigarette. "Hello, Ma," May Lee said, "I'm sorry to call you so late, but I just have to ask you something. Did my brother ever have a puppy? Did he have one when he was a little boy? Come on, Ma, I have to know."

While her mother talked, May Lee started to light her cigarette. But then her eyes grew wide. She held the lighted match, listening hard to what her mother was saying. "He *did* have a puppy? When he was five years old? Then I would have been two! What did it look like— do you remember? What did he call it? Ow!" May Lee shouted as she dropped the match into an ashtray.

"Really? He called it Brownie? What happened to it?"

May Lee listened for a moment, then turned to Sue and said excitedly, "She says they had to get rid of the dog because it kept jumping up on me and pushing me down! They couldn't get it to stay away from me!"

"Wow!" Sue said. "Then it wasn't a trick!"

"Oh, I'm sorry, Ma," May Lee was saying, "I was just talking to my friend Sue. Why didn't you ever tell me about the dog before? Oh . . . Yes . . . He felt bad about it . . ." May Lee stood looking out the window while she talked. Suddenly she said, "I'll call you back, Ma. There's something I've got to do!" She slammed down the phone and ran out the door.

"Where are you going?" Sue called as she jumped up and ran after May Lee. May Lee was already running down the stairs and out the front door of the apartment building.

A man was going by on the sidewalk, walking a big dog. May Lee ran up to him and asked, "May I pat your dog?"

The man looked surprised, but he said, "Sure, go ahead."

May Lee patted the dog carefully on the back. Then she patted it on the head and scratched it under the chin. Suddenly she jumped up and down and cheered, "Look! I can do it! I can do it!"

"That's great! Now come back inside," Sue said as she pulled May Lee back toward the building. The man looked after them, scratching his head.

"Listen, Sue, I just had a great idea!" May Lee said as they went back up the stairs. "Let's go back and see that hypnotist's show again tomorrow night. Then, when he calls for people to go up on the stage, *you* could go up and you could ask him to stop those headaches of yours!"

"Oh, no," Sue said, "I could never do that! Get up there in front of all those people and talk about my life, while I'm asleep and I don't know what I'm saying? No, I could never do that!" She yawned and reached for her coat. "Well, it's been quite a day. I've got to get home."

As she rode home on the bus, she thought about May Lee's idea. It *would* be nice to get rid of those headaches. Then she could have a lot more fun in life. But no, she shook her head. Not up there in front of all those people. She could never do that.

But May Lee didn't give up.

The next night, May Lee went back to see Lorenzo Lang's show. After the show, she went to the stage door and stood with the other people who were waiting for the hypnotist to come out. When he came out, May Lee waited for the others to get through talking to him. After everyone else had gone, she said softly, "Mr. Lang . . ."

Lang turned to look at her. "Yes? What can I do for you?"

"I . . . I wanted to thank you," May Lee began. "You got me over my fear of dogs."

"Oh, yes, last night. You were very good. Yes, *very* good. *I* should thank *you*," he said, bowing. Then he turned and started to walk away.

May Lee ran after him and called, "Mr. Lang, wait! One more thing!"

Lang stopped and looked at her. "Yes?"

"I have a friend who gets headaches—really bad ones. Can you help her?"

"Headaches? Headaches are very hard," Lang said. "There are so many things that could be causing them. No, I really don't think I could help her." He started to walk away again.

May Lee felt sad. Poor Sue. Even the great Lorenzo

Lang couldn't help her. "I know one thing that gives her headaches!" she burst out. "It's our boss, Mr. Clark! He's so mean. He yells at us all the time!"

Lang stopped and turned around slowly. "Mr. Clark? Is that . . . is that Robert Clark? Do you work for Clark's Moving and Storage Company?"

"Yes, we both work there. Do you know Mr. Clark?" May Lee asked.

"No, I don't know him," Lang said quickly. "I . . . I just saw his name on a sign. Maybe . . . Maybe I could do something for your friend after all. Here's my card. My office is only a few blocks away from where you work. Why don't you bring your friend to see me on Monday, after work? I'll be waiting for you."

Lang bowed and walked away into the night. May Lee stood looking after him, holding the card.

When Monday morning came, Sue still felt tired, but she got up and dragged herself to work. She got to the Moving and Storage Company just a few minutes before nine. She hurried into the warehouse office, took the cover off her typewriter, and got the new work orders ready to type. She wanted to get to work just in case Clark came into the office.

Just at nine, May Lee rushed through the door. She hurried over to Sue's desk, puffing quickly on one last cigarette. "Sue, I've got to talk to you!" she said. "I talked to—"

"Good morning, ladies!" a man's voice boomed. It was Clark! "I hope you both had a nice weekend. And now I hope you are well rested and *ready to go to work!*"

May Lee turned her head slowly and saw Clark standing in the office doorway. "I'll talk to you at break," she told Sue quickly. She threw her cigarette into Sue's

waiting for her. "Well, what's up?" Sue asked.

"I got you an appointment with him!" May Lee said. "With Lorenzo Lang!"

"An appointment with Lang? How? Why?"

May Lee told her all about it. "He'll be waiting for you today after work!" she told Sue excitedly.

"Oh, I couldn't . . ." Sue started to say.

"You're going!"

"I'll have to think it over."

"You're going."

The day seemed to go by very quickly. Soon Sue and May Lee were hurrying down the street to the building where Lang's office was. They went in the big front door and got into the elevator, then made their way down the hallway until they came to a door with a small sign that said

Lorenzo Lang

HYPNOTIST

May Lee pushed the doorbell, and the door opened.

May Lee walked into the office, pulling Sue behind her. The hypnotist was standing in front of them. He bowed deeply to each of them and then spoke to Sue in a quiet voice. "Your friend has told me about you and about your headaches." He smiled sadly at her. "You must be in great pain."

Sue looked into Lang's eyes—such good, kind, deep eyes. She felt that she could trust him. "Yes," she said, "the headaches *are* very bad. I have been to one doctor after another, but they can't seem to do anything for me. Can you help me?"

Lang put his hand on Sue's head and said, "As I told your friend, headaches are very hard. But I will try."

"Oh, thank you!" Sue said. May Lee's eyes were bright.

Lang put up his hand. "Do not thank me yet. It may not work. You will have to come back many times. And there will be a charge of forty dollars for every visit."

Sue blinked. Forty dollars for every visit! Oh well, it wasn't much worse than going to a doctor. If it worked it would be worth it. "Yes," she said, "that will be fine. I'll write you a check."

"Shall we start then?" Lang asked, sitting down at his desk and taking out a notebook. "I need to ask you some questions to help me get at the cause of your headaches. First, tell me about your job. Tell me what you do."

"Well, I work for Clark's Moving and Storage Company. I work in the supervisor's office, in the big warehouse. I make out the work orders for the moving vans—you know, where the men should go to pick things up, and where they should take them. I do a lot of other little things, too. For example, when a truck is all loaded, I put on the seal that makes sure the doors are kept shut until the truck gets to where it's going. Things like that."

Lang made some notes in his notebook. "Now, tell me about your boss. Your friend says that he yells at you."

"Mr. Clark? Oh, he yells at everyone. I hate him! No, that's not a very nice thing to say. But he is a hard person to get along with. If you don't do everything his way, he gets mad."

"I know, I know," Lang mumbled. He saw May Lee looking at him, so he quickly made some more notes in his notebook. "Yes, that could cause headaches. Now how long have you worked there, and where did you work before that?" Lang asked Sue some more questions, then put away his notebook and stood up. He smiled at Sue and asked, "Are you ready to be hypnotized?"

Sue took a deep breath and said, "Yes, I'm ready."

"All right, còme with me." He led them into the next room, which was quite dark, lit only by two soft lamps. The windows were covered with heavy, dark curtains, so that the sounds from the street were cut off. It was very quiet.

There was nothing in the room but a few chairs and a table. Lang led Sue to a chair that stood by itself in the middle of the room. "If you will sit here . . ." he said. "Now lean back in the chair and put your feet flat on the floor. Let your hands lie in your lap, like this." He put Sue's hands in her lap, lying with the palms up. His touch was soft and sure.

Now he smiled sadly at May Lee. "Maybe it would be better if you left," he told her. "Your friend can feel that you are here. She is shy in front of people, even you, and that will make it harder for her to let go. She will not fall into a deep trance, and then we won't be able to dig into her past to help her."

"All right," May Lee said, "whatever you say."

Lang walked her to the door. "Maybe you could wait downstairs," he told her as he closed the door behind her.

He went back to Sue, carrying a gold watch on a chain. He held the watch up in front of Sue's eyes and it began to turn slowly, catching the light, as he started to speak in a soft voice. "You see the watch turning, turning. You are very relaxed. You think of nothing. There is nothing in your mind—no thoughts, no ideas, nothing but the watch, turning and turning. Now you are getting sleepy. You are very sleepy. Let your head fall forward. Let your eyes close. Sleep."

Lang looked at Sue carefully. "She's only in a light trance," he said to himself. "I've *got* to get her into a deep trance, or she won't do what I tell her to do. She doesn't like her boss, but she wouldn't do anything to hurt him. My plan wouldn't work."

Now Sue heard the voice go on. "You are very sleepy. Your body feels very heavy. You are falling into a deep trance. Your eyes are closed. You can't open them. You are very sleepy . . ." The voice went on and on, a calm, soft sound in the quiet room.

At last the voice stopped. Lang looked closely at Sue, then took her arm and held it out in front of her. "You can't move your arm," he told her. Then he let go. Her arm stayed where he had put it.

He watched her carefully. The arm did not move.

Lang smiled and said, "At last we have done it. She is in a deep trance. Now, a plan . . ." He got a chair, sat down in front of Sue, and thought for a long time. "Listen carefully," he said at last. "Tomorrow you will go to work, just as always. But when it is time to go home, you will leave your checkbook in your desk. You will take your pocketbook, but you will leave your checkbook at work. Do you understand?"

"Yes."

"At eight o'clock, you will see that you do not have your checkbook. You will go back to the office to get it. When you go in, you will leave the warehouse door unlocked. You will go into the office and stay there for one hour. You will not come out."

"Yes."

"At the end of one hour," Lang went on, "you will come back out into the warehouse. You will go to the loading dock. You will see that the seal has been cut on one of the loaded vans. You will put on a new seal."

"Yes."

"Then you will go home again. And you will not remember that you were at the warehouse. You will not remember anything that has happened here today. But you will do what I have told you to do."

Lang stood up. He put his chair back by the table, then walked over to Sue and put her arm down. "Sue, when I count to five, you will wake up," he said. "You will feel as if you have had a good rest. You will feel better, even if you still have headaches. You will feel that I can help you. You will want to come back to me. Now . . . one . . . two . . . three . . . four . . . five!"

Sue lifted her head. She opened her eyes and blinked. She looked around for a moment, then she smiled at Lang. "What happened?" she asked.

"You have been in a deep trance," Lang said. "You have done very well."

"Did you find out why I get headaches?" Sue asked hopefully.

"No," Lang said, "but I feel that we will find out

soon. Maybe in the next appointment, or the one after that. I want you to come back at the same time next week."

"All right," Sue said. She stood up slowly, holding onto her chair. "Oh, I feel so dizzy!"

"That will be forty dollars," Lang told her.

"Oh, yes," Sue said sleepily, "I'll write you a check." She wrote out the check and gave it to him. She said, "Thank you," and walked slowly out of the office.

Lang stood looking at Sue's check. "She never said a word when I told her how much I would charge her. It's too bad I didn't say sixty dollars!"

He walked over to the window and pulled back the curtain. On the street below him, he could see May Lee and Sue just going out the front door of the building. "Well, Sue," he said to himself, "maybe I can help you get at the cause of your headaches. I don't know. But I do know that you will help *me* get rid of *mine*."

He watched the women walk up the sidewalk to the bus stop. "I'll get him," Lang mumbled. "One way or another, I'll get him."

Directions. Answer these questions about the chapter you have just read. Put an *x* in the box beside the best answer to each question.

1. (B) Why did May Lee's brother have to get rid of his dog?

   ☐ a. It kept pushing little May Lee down.
   ☐ b. It kept hurting people.
   ☐ c. It barked too much.
   ☐ d. His mother didn't like it.

2. (C) What did May Lee do right after she talked to her mother on the phone?

   ☐ a. She lit a cigarette.
   ☐ b. She dropped a match into an ashtray.
   ☐ c. She ran out of her apartment.
   ☐ d. She told Sue that her brother had had to get rid of his dog.

3. (D) Why didn't Sue want to go up on the stage to be hypnotized?

   ☐ a. She was too shy.
   ☐ b. She didn't trust Lang.
   ☐ c. She was afraid that she would fall off the stage.
   ☐ d. She was afraid that she would be late for work.

4. (B) How did May Lee get Sue an appointment with Lang?

- ☐ a. She called Lang at his office.
- ☐ b. She waited for Lang at the stage door.
- ☐ c. She asked Clark to talk to Lang.
- ☐ d. She talked to Lang while she was on the stage.

5. (A) Lang told May Lee, "Maybe I could do something for your friend after all. *Here's my card.*" Why did he say that?

- ☐ a. He wanted to play cards with May Lee.
- ☐ b. The card told May Lee his name, his address, and his job.
- ☐ c. He wanted May Lee to tell him what the card said.
- ☐ d. May Lee had dropped her own card.

6. (E) Why did May Lee want Sue to go to Lang's office?

- ☐ a. Sue had never seen a hypnotist.
- ☐ b. Sue had to write Lang a check.
- ☐ c. May Lee wanted all her friends to see him.
- ☐ d. May Lee felt that Lang could help Sue get rid of her headaches.

7. (E) Why did Lang want to hypnotize Sue?

- ☐ a. He wanted her to be in his show.
- ☐ b. He wanted to help her get over her fear of dogs.
- ☐ c. He wanted to use her in his plan to hurt someone.
- ☐ d. He just wanted to help her to relax.

8. (A) In Lang's office, the sounds from the street *were cut off*. What does that mean?

 ☐ a. No sounds could be heard from outside.
 ☐ b. The windows were broken.
 ☐ c. The street had been closed to cars.
 ☐ d. Cars could be heard going by outside.

9. (D) Why did Lang send May Lee downstairs?

 ☐ a. She wanted to smoke a cigarette.
 ☐ b. He didn't want her to hear what he was going to tell Sue.
 ☐ c. He was afraid that she would talk while he was hypnotizing Sue.
 ☐ d. He was afraid that she would not want him to hypnotize Sue.

10. (C) Which of these things did Lang tell Sue to do first?

 ☐ a. Go back to the warehouse.
 ☐ b. Put a new seal on the truck.
 ☐ c. Go home from work.
 ☐ d. Leave her checkbook in her desk.

Skills Used to Answer Questions
A. Recognizing Words in Context   B. Recalling Facts
C. Keeping Events in Order   D. Making Inferences
E. Understanding Main Ideas

Roots Ending in e

In the last chapter you learned that you can make new words from roots and suffixes. You also learned that sometimes a spelling change must be made to make the new word. Now you will learn about the spelling changes that must be made when the root ends in the letter *e.*

Every letter in the alphabet is either a vowel or a consonant. The letters *a, e, i, o, u,* and sometimes *y* are vowels. All the other letters in the alphabet are consonants.

Look at the roots and suffixes below.

arrive + -al

write + -ing

You can see that both *arrive* and *write* end in the letter *e.* Now look at the suffixes. Both begin with vowels. The first suffix, -*al,* begins with the vowel *a.* The second suffix, -*ing,* begins with the vowel *i.* Here is how to make new words from these roots and suffixes.

arrive + -al = arrival

write + -ing = writing

There is a spelling change in the new words. The final *e* was dropped from the root. Then the suffix was added. In the first example, the final *e* was dropped from *arrive.* The suffix -*al* was then added. The new word is *arrival.* In the second example, the final *e* in *write* was dropped. Then the suffix -*ing* was added. The new word is *writing.*

When adding suffixes that begin with consonants,

however, the rule is different. When adding such a suffix to a root that ends with *e,* there is no spelling change. Look below at the roots and suffixes and the new words made from them.

hope + -ful = hopeful

pave + -ment = pavement

Hope and *pave* both end in the letter *e.* Both suffixes begin with consonants. The suffix *-ful* begins with the consonant *f.* The suffix *-ment* begins with the consonant *m.* There are no spelling changes in the new words *hopeful* and *pavement.*

Spelling Rule #1: When a root ends in the letter *e,* and the suffix begins with a vowel, drop the final *e* from the root. Then add the suffix.

Exercise 1

Make new words from the roots and suffixes given below. All the roots end in the letter *e.* All the suffixes begin with vowels. Drop the final *e* from each root. Then add the suffix. Print the new word on the line provided. The first one has been done for you.

1. skate + -ing ___skating___

2. survive + -al _____

3. give + -ing _____

4. dictate + -or _____

5. change + -ed _____

6. come + -ing _____

7. give + -en _____

8. smoke + -er _____

Exercise 2

Look at the pairs of roots and suffixes given below. All the roots end in the letter *e*. Some of the suffixes begin with vowels, some begin with consonants. Make new words from the roots and suffixes. Follow these steps:

1. Look at the suffix. If it begins with a vowel, print *V* in the box next to it. If it begins with a consonant, print *C* in the box next to it.
2. Put the root and the suffix together to make a word. If you have printed *C* in the box, just add the suffix to the root. If you have printed *V* in the box, drop the final *e* from the root before adding the suffix.
3. Print the new word on the line provided.

The first two have been done for you as examples.

1. pure + -ify   [V] _purify_____

2. hope + -less   [C] _hopeless_____

3. hope + -ing   [ ] _____

4. care + -less ☐ _____

5. care + -ing ☐ _____

6. care + -ful ☐ _____

7. engage + -ing ☐ _____

8. engage + -ment ☐ _____

9. use + -ful ☐ _____

10. use + -ing ☐ _____

11. love + -ing ☐ _____

12. love + -less ☐ _____

Wage and Tax Statement

You know employers must withhold part of each worker's earnings to pay for the person's income taxes and Social Security (FICA). A worker's paycheck stub is a record of how much money the person has earned and how much has been withheld from each check. In January of each year, employers must give each of their workers a *Wage and Tax Statement*. The statement is Form W-2, from the Internal Revenue Service. It is a statement of how much money the worker earned and of the tax deductions that were made from the worker's earnings between January 1 and December 31 of the year that just ended. A W-2 form is shown below.

1 Control number					
		OMB No. 1545-0008			
2 Employer's name, address, and ZIP code			3 Employer's identification number 95-22125683		4 Employer's State number 214-5176-0
Franklin Company 740 Royal Drive Reno, Nevada 89504			5 Stat. employee ☐ Deceased Legal rep ☐	942 emp ☐ Subtotal ☐	Void ☐
			6 Allocated tips		7 Advance EIC payment
8 Employee's social security number 572-19-4627	9 Federal income tax withheld $5,913.60		10 Wages, tips, other compensation $30,000.00		11 Social security tax withheld $2010.00
12 Employee's name, address, and ZIP code			13 Social security wages $30,000.00		14 Social security tips
Janet Clarke 26 Lincoln Ave. Reno, Nevada 89504			16		
			17 State income tax $420.00	18 State wages, tips, etc.	19 Name of State Nevada
			20 Local income tax	21 Local wages, tips, etc.	22 Name of locality

Form **W-2 Wage and Tax Statement** **1984** Copy C For employee's records
This information is being furnished to the Internal Revenue Service

Department of the Treasury
Internal Revenue Service

A W-2 form gives the following information:

1. The employer's name and address. (The employer is the company or group that the taxpayer works for.)
2. The worker's name, address and Social Security number.
3. The amount of the worker's total earnings for the year. (The worker in the example earned $30,000.00)
4. The amount of the worker's earnings that were withheld for federal income tax. (The worker in the example on the left had $5,913.60 withheld for federal income tax.)
5. The amount of Social Security tax (FICA) withheld from the worker's earnings. (In the example that amount is $2,010.00.)
6. The amount of the worker's earnings that were withheld for state and local taxes. (The worker in the example had $420.00 withheld for state taxes. Nothing was withheld for local taxes.)

People need their W-2 forms to fill out their income tax returns. Every worker must file an income tax return with the federal government each year between January 1 and April 15. It tells the government how much the worker should have paid in income taxes for the year.

To fill out a tax return, you need to know your total earnings (box 10). You also need to know how much money was withheld from your earnings for federal income tax (box 9).

A worker is given three copies of his or her W-2 form. One copy is to be sent in with the person's federal income tax return. One is to be sent along with the state income tax return. The last is for the person's own records.

Keeping Records of Other Income

You know that a W-2 form is a statement of wages earned and taxes withheld over a whole year. A worker gets a W-2 statement from his or her employer. But sometimes people earn money in ways other than from their regular jobs. Taxes must be paid on that income too.

Many people earn interest on money that they have in savings accounts. Some people do work for people who are not their regular employers. They might do odd jobs or house repairs for people. They might do a short-term job now and then for a company. A person must pay taxes on all earnings.

But what kinds of records are there for those kinds of earnings? Well, once a year, banks send statements to their customers, telling them how much interest they earned on their accounts during the year. Such a statement is often called a *statement of payment*. Statements of payment are also often sent out at the end of the year by companies that hire people to do short-term or one-time jobs. For odd jobs, however, there is usually no kind of record or statement given. It is up to the worker to keep track of all earnings and to report those earnings on his or her income tax return.

A statement of payment from a company is shown on the next page.

		OMB. No 1545—0116 Statement for Recipients of
Nordic Press 2545 Bayview Ave. San Francisco, CA 91340	Type or print PAYER'S name, address, ZIP code	**1984** Nonemployee Compensation

Recipient's social security number	1 Fees, commissions, and other compensation
621-43-4651	$1,250.00

Type or print RECIPIENT'S name, address and ZIP code below.	
Philip Matera 10 Mission St. San Francisco, CA 91345	**This information is being furnished to the Internal Revenue Service.**

Form **1099—NEC** ✩U.S. GOVERNMENT PRINTING OFFICE 1983-390-295 E.I. #36-2705514   Department of the Treasury—Internal Revenue Service

A statement of payment gives the following information:

1. Name and address of the company or bank
2. Name and address of the person to whom payment was made
3. Social Security number of the person to whom payment was made
4. The amount paid

Such statements give you information you need to figure the amount of federal taxes you owe. You get only one copy of such a statement. You keep it for your own records. The government gets its copy from the bank or company.

Reading Statements of Earnings

You know that the government withholds part of a person's job earnings for taxes. Each year a worker is given a *Wage and Tax Statement,* also known as a W-2 form. That form contains information that the worker needs to fill out his or her federal income tax return.

You also know that a person must pay taxes on all money earned. So if a person earned money doing jobs other than his or her regular job, or from interest on savings accounts, that income must be reported to the government. Taxes must be paid on that income. For interest earnings and for some short-term or one-time jobs for a company, a person will receive a statement of payment. But for many kinds of small jobs, no statement will be given. The worker must keep track of all such earnings. All earnings must be reported on a person's federal income tax return.

Exercise 1

On the next page is a sample *Wage and Tax Statement,* or W-2 form. Use the information on the form to answer the questions that follow. The questions ask for the information that a person needs to figure his or her taxes. Find the information on the statement, and copy it in the spaces provided.

1 Control number		OMB No. 1545-0008		

2 Employer's name, address, and ZIP code	3 Employer's identification number	4 Employer's State number
Quick Copy Printing Company 115 Main St. Richmond, VA 23229	36-13591284	214-5176-0

5 Stat employee ☐	Deceased ☐	Legal rep. ☐	942 emp. ☐	Subtotal ☐	Void ☐

6 Allocated tips	7 Advance EIC payment

8 Employee's social security number	9 Federal income tax withheld	10 Wages, tips, other compensation	11 Social security tax withheld
183-45-9632	$1,990.00	$12,400.00	$830.00

12 Employee's name, address, and ZIP code	13 Social security wages	14 Social security tips
Anita George 35 Hill Drive Richmond, VA 23229	$12,400.00	

16			
17 State income tax	18 State wages, tips, etc.	19 Name of State Virginia
20 Local income tax	21 Local wages, tips, etc.	22 Name of locality

Form **W-2 Wage and Tax Statement** **1984** Copy C For employee's records
This information is being furnished to the Internal Revenue Service
Department of the Treasury
Internal Revenue Service

1. How much money did this person earn in 1984?

_____

2. How much of the person's earnings was withheld for federal income tax?

_____

3. How much of the person's earnings was withheld for state income tax?

_____

4. What is the person's Social Security number?

_____

5. How much of the person's earnings was withheld for Social Security tax (FICA)?

_____

Exercise 2

A statement of interest earnings from a bank is shown below. Use the statement to answer the questions that follow. The questions ask for the information that is needed when filing a tax return. Find the information on the statement, and copy it on the lines provided.

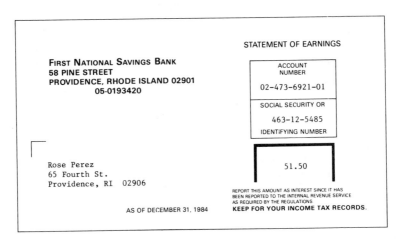

1. What is the name of the bank that sent the statement?

   _____

2. What is the name of the person who has the account?

   _____

3. How much interest did the person earn on the account for the year?

   _____

3
The Plan

Study the words in the box. Then read the sentences below with your teacher. Look carefully at the words in boldface type.

afternoon	bothers	facing	nervous
awful	carrying	family	pretty
beginning	easier	hungry	reason
believe	else	keys	report
blankets	evening	kitchen	silver

1. I've got to get my bus and get home. I'm **hungry**!
2. She went to the **kitchen** to get some supper.
3. **Report** back to me tomorrow.
4. Just as she did every **afternoon**, Sue put away her papers.
5. She got up and got her **keys** to the office.
6. The two men filled their bag with the **silver**.
7. They put the **blankets** back over the other things in the truck.
8. She still hasn't moved! I can't **believe** it!
9. What a way to spend an **evening**—watching TV.
10. The men put down what they were **carrying**.
11. He set the chair down in front of Sue and sat down, **facing** her.
12. Is it Clark that **bothers** you?
13. Well, what **else** could it be?
14. Has someone in your **family** lost a job?
15. That was **easier** than I thought it would be.
16. It went **pretty** well today.
17. He said I was **beginning** to open up.
18. Mr. Clark is just as **awful** as ever.
19. But the **reason** I called, Dad . . . Can I come over?
20. The man's voice sounded **nervous**.

May Lee was waiting for Sue downstairs in Lang's office building when the elevator opened, and Sue walked slowly out. May Lee ran up to her asking, "How did it go? What happened? Did you get hypnotized?"

"I don't remember a thing," Sue said. "I just feel so sleepy . . ."

"You do sound kind of funny," May Lee told her. "So you must have done it! You *were* hypnotized!"

"Yes, he said I was in a deep trance. And I feel better already. I feel . . . well, I feel rested."

"That's great!" May Lee said. "Isn't Lang just the greatest?"

"Yes. I just wish he didn't charge so much."

"But it's worth it, isn't it?"

"Oh yes," Sue said. She touched May Lee's arm and added, "Thank you for getting me to come."

"I'm glad it worked out. Now I've got to get my bus and get home. I'm hungry!" May Lee said.

Sue looked at her watch and said, "Oh, I didn't know it was so late!" They hurried out of the building and walked down the street to the bus stop.

When Sue got home, she hung up her coat, then walked around her apartment trying to think what to do next. She went into the kitchen to get some supper, but somehow she wasn't hungry. At last she gave up and went to bed.

The next morning, Sue was at work bright and early. She still felt so happy that she didn't mind being at work at all.

As Sue sat down at her desk, Lang was in his office

talking to two men. "Tonight, at Clark's Moving and Storage," he told them, "you wait across the street. At about half past eight, a woman will come and open the warehouse. She'll go in and leave the door open. You go to the loading dock, find a moving van that's all set to go, and cut off the seal. Take a few things off the van and close it back up. Then go home."

"OK. What do you want us to do with the stuff from the truck?" one of the men asked.

"I don't care. Keep it," Lang said.

"What if the woman sees us?" the other man asked.

"She won't."

"If you say so," the first man said.

"Report back to me tomorrow," Lang said. "If all goes well, there will be more jobs. Here is half your pay— you will get the other half tomorrow." Lang handed each of them a $100 bill. "You may go now." He sat down at his desk and started to write in his notebook.

"What a job!" one of the men said as they went out. "We don't even have to break in—some woman lets us in. We pick out some stuff, then we get to keep the stuff, and we get paid too!"

"That Lang is kind of strange," the other man said. "What do you think he's up to?"

"Who cares? Let's go," the first man said. They got into the elevator and pushed the button.

At Clark's Moving and Storage, the day went by quietly. Clark didn't come out into the warehouse, and Sue got her work orders done quickly. Two trucks were filled and ready to go out in the morning. Sue put the seals on them, then went back to her desk.

At last it was five o'clock, quitting time. Just as she had done every afternoon for three years, Sue put away her papers and put the cover on her typewriter. She put on her coat and picked up her pocketbook.

But suddenly she stopped. Her face had a strange, sleepy look. Slowly she took her checkbook out of her pocketbook and put it into her desk. Then she turned and walked slowly out of the office.

When she got outside, she felt more awake. She went home, had supper, then sat down to watch TV. It was a night like any other night.

But at eight o'clock, everything changed. The sleepy look came over her face again. She got up, put on her coat, got her keys to the office, and walked out of her apartment without looking back.

Soon she was walking down the dark street toward the warehouse, looking straight ahead of her. She didn't

see the two men standing across the street as she unlocked the door of the warehouse. She walked straight to the supervisor's office and went in.

The two men crossed the street and looked in through the open warehouse door. They stepped carefully inside, closing the door behind them. "Where is she?" one man asked the other.

"There's a light on in that room. She must be in there," the other man said, pointing at the office door. "Let's go."

They turned on their flashlights and made their way to the loading dock. Two moving vans stood there, ready to go in the morning. They cut the seal of one of the trucks and opened the doors. They shined their flashlights on the things inside, all covered with blankets.

"You pick out some things," the first man said. "I want to check on the woman." He turned off his flashlight and walked quietly toward the office door. Carefully he peeked in and watched Sue for a while. Then he hurried back to the truck.

"You should see her!" he told the other man. "She's just sitting there. She never moved in all the time I was looking at her—just sat there, looking at the wall. I don't like this at all!"

"Don't worry about it," the other man said. "Didn't you see the sign on Lang's door? He's a hypnotist! He must have hypnotized her. Now let's get moving. I found some silver on the truck. I'll hand it down to you, and you put it in the bag."

The two men filled their bag with silver. Then they put the blankets back over the other things in the truck, stepped out of the truck, and closed the doors. They walked quietly toward the warehouse door.

The first man stopped for a moment and looked back toward the office. "She still hasn't moved," he said. "I can't believe it. Just keep that hypnotist away from *me!*" he added as he hurried out the door after the other man.

The two men had been in the warehouse for only ten minutes. Now the warehouse was quiet and dark. But Sue did not move. For fifty more minutes, she sat and looked at the wall. Then, just an hour after she had come in, she stood up. Holding her checkbook, she walked out of the office and closed the door. She walked straight across the dark warehouse and put a new seal on the truck. Then she walked out of the warehouse and locked the door. Looking straight in front of her, she walked slowly home.

When she got home, the TV was still on. She hung up her coat and sat down to watch TV. Bit by bit, the strange look left her face. At last she yawned and got up. "Ten o'clock, time for bed," she told herself. "What a way to spend an evening—just watching TV."

The next morning, when the moving van pulled out of the warehouse, no one saw that it had a new seal. And Sue did not remember being at the warehouse the night before.

It took two days for the van to get to the place where it would be unloaded. So it was two days before anyone knew that the van had been robbed.

Clark burst into the warehouse shouting, "All right, everyone get over here!" He was red in the face, and his eyes were bugging out. "I mean everyone! Get out here this minute!"

The men on the loading dock put down what they were carrying and came running. The supervisor jumped up from his desk. "Come on, Sue," he said as he headed for the door, "the old grouch has really lost his cool this time. Something must have happened!"

As Sue followed him out into the warehouse, she could feel a headache starting up. Everything had been going so well, too!

"What happened, Mr. Clark?" the supervisor asked.

"That's what *I* want to know!" Clark shouted. "A truck went out of here two days ago. I just got a call—all the silver that was on that truck is gone! And I want to know why!"

"Maybe someone broke into the truck while it was parked somewhere," someone said.

"No, the seal had not been cut. So it happened right here in this warehouse, while the truck was being loaded! It was one of you!" Clark turned around and looked right at Sue.

"Sue, I want to know who worked on that truck, everyone who was near it before it was sealed. Here's the job number. Now get those work orders!"

Sue ran into the office, got out the work orders, and took them to Clark. Clark and the supervisor went over the work orders carefully. Sue could hear Clark yelling at the supervisor.

Later, the supervisor came back into the office. "That man makes me so mad!" he told Sue. "Something happens and he blames it on us! He asked each of the men all kinds of questions. I'll bet he thinks we're *all* robbers! I don't think that silver was ever on the truck!"

Sue just sat with her head in her hands, looking down at her desk. Her head was pounding. She couldn't wait until next Monday, when she would go back to see Lang.

Monday came, and Sue went back to see the hypnotist. As she walked in the front door of the building where

Lang's office was, she felt happy. But she was scared, too.

She pushed the button for the elevator, and the elevator door opened like a big mouth. Sue took a deep breath and stepped in.

Lang met her at his office door and led her into the other room. The door closed behind them.

It was very dark in the room, and so quiet. Sue could almost *feel* the quiet around her. "Sit down," Lang said in a soft voice, and Sue sat down in the chair in the middle of the room. Lang stood by the curtains at the side of the room, where Sue could hardly see him.

It was very quiet. Sue tried to relax, but she still felt a little bit scared.

At last Lang began to talk quietly, in a voice that seemed to fill the room. "Close your eyes and relax. Relax every part of your body. Start with your feet. Think about your toes. Relax your toes . . ." The calm voice went on and on until Sue felt more relaxed than she had ever felt before. All her fears seemed to melt away.

Lang held up the gold watch, and Sue watched it turning, turning, while the quiet voice went on and on. "Your eyes are getting heavy. You are very sleepy. You can't move your body . . ." This time it did not take so long. When Lang took Sue's arm and held it out in front of her, it stayed stiff, right where he had put it. Sue was in a deep trance.

"OK, let's get to work," Lang said. He walked over to the table, got another chair, and set it down in front of Sue. He sat down facing her and leaned back with his hands behind his head. "These headaches of yours—how long have you had them?" he asked.

"Five years," Sue said in a flat voice.

"OK, five years. Now, how long have you been working? Five years?"

"Yes."

"That was a lucky break! So working gives you a headache, does it? Is it working for Clark that gives you a headache? Is it Clark that bothers you?"

"No," Sue said.

"It would bother me!" Lang said. "Well, what else could it be? Are you afraid that you will lose your job?"

"Yes," Sue said.

"You are? Now, why—" Lang mumbled. "Have you ever lost a job?" he asked Sue.

"No."

"Has someone in your family lost a job?"

"Yes."

"Now we're getting somewhere. Did your father lose his job?"

"No," Sue said. Then she said, "Yes."

"Rats!" Lang said to himself. "This was going so well, too. No, then yes. What does that mean? Wait a minute . . ." He asked Sue, "Did your father lose his job a long time ago?"

"Yes."

"When you were a little girl? How old were you?"

"Three," Sue said.

"Full of lucky breaks today! OK, Sue, you are now three years old. Your father has just lost his job. What is happening?"

Sue's face changed, and she began to cry. "Mama, don't leave! Mama!" she cried in a little girl's voice. "Papa didn't mean to lose his job. He'll get another one! He said he would! He'll keep it, too! Oh, Mama, don't leave us!" Sue was crying hard now. "She's gone! My mama is gone! She doesn't love us anymore!"

Lang reached out and touched Sue on the arm. "It's all right now," he said. "You are grown up now. It's all over." Sue stopped crying, just as suddenly as she had started. She sat still, her eyes closed, her arm held out in front of her.

"So you're afraid, aren't you?" Lang asked her. "You're afraid that if you lose your job no one will love you? You're afraid that your family will leave you, the way your mother left your father?"

"Yes."

"But your father never left you, did he?"

"No."

"He got another job," Lang went on, "and he took care of you, didn't he?"

"Yes."

"He will always be around when you need him, because he loves you. He is not like your mother. He will always love you, no matter what happens. You are grown up now, and you know that. Right?"

"Yes," Sue said, "he loves me, no matter what happens."

Lang sat back again. "That was so much easier than I thought it would be. What a lucky day. But now I've got to set it up so that she will keep on coming back," he said to himself as he got up and walked around the room. "I've got to say this just right. I think I've got it." He went back and sat down in front of Sue.

"I am going to tell you some things," he said to Sue. "You will not remember that I said them, but you will do as I say. First, you will feel better this week. You will feel happy and full of hope. You will go to see your father."

"Yes, I will do that," Sue said.

"Next, you will feel that I have helped you, but you will still feel that I could help you more. You will want to come back."

"Yes, I will come back," Sue said.

"Tomorrow you will leave your checkbook at work

again, then you will go home and stay there until eight o'clock. At eight you will go back to the warehouse, just as you did last week. You will leave the door open. You will go into the supervisor's office to get your checkbook."

Lang sat back in his chair and stared at Sue. It seemed as if there was something else he should say just then, but he couldn't think of it. So he went on, "You will seal the truck again. Then you will go home. You will not remember that you have been there. Do you understand?"

"Yes."

Lang looked at Sue for a moment, deep in thought. Then he said, "When I count to five, you will wake up. One . . . two . . . three . . . four . . . five!"

Sue's arm dropped slowly into her lap. She opened her eyes and smiled hopefully at Lang. "Did you find anything out?" she asked. "Did you find out why I get the headaches?"

Lang smiled down at her, but he said, "No, not yet. These things can't be hurried. But you did a lot of talking this time. You are really starting to open up, and I feel that we will find out soon. You will come back next week at the same time?"

"Yes, I will," Sue said. "I'll write you a check."

Lang walked Sue to the door, then went to the window to watch her as she went down the street to the bus stop. He watched her until the bus came and took her away. "It is going well," he said to himself. "When that truck was robbed last week, Mr. Robert Clark must have been really mad. If I know him, he has been yelling at everyone ever since. But wait until it happens again! He won't be the only one to be mad. The word will begin to get around. Then it will happen again and again. No one will want to use Clark's Moving and Storage Company. They won't let Robert *near* their things." Lang turned away from the window. "And then—at last—we will be even."

When Sue got home the phone was ringing. When she picked it up she heard May Lee's voice asking excitedly, "How did it go today?"

"Pretty well, I think," Sue told her. "He said I was beginning to open up."

"So he still didn't find out why you have headaches?"

"No," Sue said, "not yet."

"Oh well, keep trying. Mr. Lang is just the greatest—"

But Sue wasn't listening. "You know what?" she said suddenly. "I was just thinking about my father. I haven't seen him in a long time, and I miss him! I'm going to give him a call. Maybe I'll go see him tomorrow."

"But I thought you didn't get along with your stepmother!" May Lee said. "You always said—"

"I *don't* get along with her, but that shouldn't keep me from seeing my own father. Listen, I'm going to call him right now. I'll see you tomorrow, OK?"

"OK," May Lee said in a surprised voice, "good-bye."

When Sue called her father, he was surprised and glad to hear from her. "How's my little girl?" he asked. "What have you been up to lately?"

"I'm fine, Dad," Sue said. "I'm still working at the warehouse. Mr. Clark is just as awful as ever. Other than that, nothing much has happened. But the reason I called, Dad . . ." she went on, "Can I come over sometime soon?"

"Sure!" her father said. "Why don't you come for supper tomorrow night?"

"Tomorrow night . . . ?" The strange, sleepy look passed over Sue's face again. "No, I can't make it tomorrow night. How about the next night?"

"Fine."

"It will be good to see you, Dad," Sue said.

The next day things were going better at Clark's Moving and Storage. Clark had begun to quiet down about the missing silver, and all the workers were feeling better. Sue had lunch with May Lee. It seemed like a normal day.

At five o'clock, Sue put on her coat and got ready to go home. But as she picked up her pocketbook, her face suddenly got that strange, sleepy look again. She put her checkbook back into her desk, then walked slowly out of the office and went home.

At eight o'clock, she got up and went out. Soon she was heading toward the warehouse again, walking slowly down the dark, quiet street, looking straight ahead. The two men were waiting across the street, watching Sue as she walked stiffly along the front of the warehouse.

"I don't know. She gives me the creeps," one of the men said.

"Don't look at her then," the other man said. But his voice sounded nervous too.

Sue unlocked the door of the warehouse and went in. She went right into the supervisor's office and took her checkbook out of the desk. For a moment she just stood and looked at the wall.

The two men had stepped into the warehouse. They walked quickly to the loading dock and broke the seal on one of the loaded vans. They opened the back of the van, got up into it, and started to take off the covers.

"Wait! What's that?" one of the men said. They turned quickly and looked toward the office.

The door was opening.

Sue stood in the doorway, looking out into the warehouse. Then she slowly stepped out of the office and began to walk across the warehouse floor.

"She sees us!" the first man said, pulling a gun out of his coat pocket. "I'll nail her!"

"No, wait!" the other man said. "She's hypnotized,

remember? She can't see us!" He grabbed some small boxes and threw them into his bag.

The first man kept his gun ready. "Let's get out of here!" he said. "Never mind the job! Let's go!"

"It's OK! Come on!" the other man said. He was working fast, grabbing any small thing he could reach and throwing it into the bag.

Sue walked slowly toward them.

The first man jumped down from the truck. He grabbed the other man by the belt and pulled him down out of the truck. He grabbed the bag and pushed the other man around the side of the truck.

Sue walked slowly up to the truck, closed the doors, and put a new seal on them. Then she turned and walked toward the warehouse door, slowly, looking straight ahead. The two men never took their eyes off her. Now she was almost all the way to the door, with her keys in her hand. "She's going to cut us off!" the first man said. He raised his gun and pointed it at Sue.

"No, wait!" the other man said.

"But she'll lock us in!" The man pointed the gun at Sue's back and started to squeeze the trigger.

"Don't do it!" the other man said, pushing the gun away. "She can't hurt us. Run!" As he spoke, he ran for the warehouse door.

The man with the gun stopped for a moment. He looked down at his gun, and then at Sue. He watched the other man run in front of Sue, and out the door. Then he ran too.

Sue didn't blink as the two men ran past her. She walked straight to the door and stepped out into the street. Then she locked up the warehouse and walked slowly home.

Directions. Answer these questions about the chapter you have just read. Put an *x* in the box beside the best answer to each question.

1. (E) Why did Lang pay the two men to rob the trucks?

   □ a. He wanted the things that were on the trucks.
   □ b. He wanted to hypnotize the two men for his show.
   □ c. He knew that the men needed money.
   □ d. He wanted to hurt Clark and his company.

2. (B) While the men robbed the truck the first time, what did Sue do for an hour?

   □ a. She sat in the office and looked at the wall.
   □ b. She helped the men take things out of the truck.
   □ c. She put new seals on all the trucks.
   □ d. She talked to Lang on the phone.

3. (C) After the men robbed the first truck, what happened next?

   □ a. Clark found out that the silver was missing.
   □ b. Clark yelled at the men on the loading dock.
   □ c. The van pulled out of the warehouse.
   □ d. Sue went home and watched TV.

4. (A) As Lang began to hypnotize her, Sue felt very relaxed. *All her fears seemed to melt away.* What does that mean?

☐ a. She wasn't afraid anymore.
☐ b. Her fears turned into water.
☐ c. It was so hot in the room that she thought she would melt.
☐ d. She was so afraid that she wanted to run away.

5. (E) What was the main reason that Sue got headaches?

☐ a. Clark kept yelling at her.
☐ b. She was afraid that she would go hungry if she lost her job.
☐ c. She was afraid that no one would love her if she lost her job.
☐ d. She hated to type work orders.

6. (D) Why did Lang tell Sue that he had not found out why she got headaches?

☐ a. He couldn't get her to go into a deep trance.
☐ b. He wanted to keep using her to unlock Clark's warehouse.
☐ c. He wasn't sure she was ready to hear the truth.
☐ d. He was afraid that she would be mad if he told her.

7. (A) Lang said, "When another truck is robbed, people will get mad. *The word will begin to get around.*" What did he mean?

- [ ] a. Lang would tell people about Clark's temper.
- [ ] b. Many people would find out that Clark's trucks were getting robbed.
- [ ] c. The truck would go around the block.
- [ ] d. Clark would go around the warehouse talking to his workers.

8. (D) Why did Sue say she couldn't go to her father's house the next night?

- [ ] a. Lang had told her to go to the warehouse the next night.
- [ ] b. Lang had told her to stay away from her father.
- [ ] c. She was going to have supper at May Lee's apartment the next night.
- [ ] d. She didn't want to see her father.

9. (C) On the second night the men came to the warehouse, which of these things happened last?

- [ ] a. Sue stepped out of the office.
- [ ] b. One of the men pointed his gun at Sue.
- [ ] c. The two men ran out of the warehouse.
- [ ] d. Sue put a new seal on the truck.

10. (B) Why did the robber want to shoot Sue?

    ☐ a. He thought she looked strange.
    ☐ b. He thought that she could see him.
    ☐ c. He wanted to show how good he was with a gun.
    ☐ d. Lang hypnotized him and told him to do it.

Skills Used to Answer Questions

A. Recognizing Words in Context   B. Recalling Facts
C. Keeping Events in Order   D. Making Inferences
E. Understanding Main Ideas

The Suffix -able

You have learned that you can make new words by adding suffixes to root words. Sometimes you must change the spelling of the root a little to make the new word. To combine a root that ends in *e* with a suffix that begins with a vowel, you must drop the final *e* from the root.

In this lesson you will learn about the suffix *-able.* *-Able* begins with the vowel *a.* Suppose you want to add *-able* to a root word that ends in *e.* The rule you have learned tells you to drop the *e* before adding the suffix. Look at the roots, suffixes and new words below.

love + -able = lovable

prove + -able = provable

In the first example you drop the *e* in *love,* then add *-able.* The new word is *lovable.* In the second example, you drop the *e* in *prove* and then add *-able.* The new word is *provable.*

Now look at the roots, suffixes and new words below.

package + -able = packageable

trace + -able = traceable

In the first example, you do *not* drop the *e* in *package* before you add the ending *-able.* In the second example, you do *not* drop the *e* in *trace* before adding the ending *-able.*

Look at the last two examples again. What letter comes before the final *e* in *package?* What letter comes before the final *e* in *trace?* A *g* comes before the final *e* in *package*. A *c* comes before the final *e* in *trace*. When a *c* or a *g* comes before the final *e* in a root word, do *not* drop the *e* before adding the suffix -*able*.

Spelling Rule #2: If a root word ends in *ce* or *ge*, do not drop the final *e* when adding the suffix -*able*.

Exercise 1

A number of words that end in *ce* or *ge* are given below. Add the suffix -*able* to each root. Remember that there is no spelling change when you add -*able* to a word that ends in *ce* or *ge*. Print each new word on the line next to the root. The first one has been done for you as an example.

1. manage   *manageable*

2. trace _____

3. notice _____

4. change _____

5. service _____

Exercise 2

A list of roots is given below. Add the suffix *-able* to each root to make a new word. Drop the final *e* before you add *-able,* unless the root ends in *ce* or *ge.* Print the new word on the line to the right of the root. The first two have been done for you.

1. value __*valuable*__

2. dance __*danceable*__

3. quote _____

4. pronounce _____

5. live _____

6. note _____

7. charge _____

8. store _____

9. exchange _____

10. move _____

Exercise 3

A list of roots and suffixes is given below. Add the endings to the roots to make new words. Remember the two rules you have learned about spelling changes:

1. If the root ends in *e* and the suffix begins with a vowel, drop the *e*. Then add the suffix.
2. If the root ends in *ce* or *ge* and the suffix is *-able,* make no spelling change. Just add the suffix to the root.

Print the new word on the line provided. The first two have been done for you as examples.

1. place + -ing ___placing___

2. place + -able ___placeable___

3. adore + -ing _____

4. adore + -able _____

5. erase + -ed _____

6. erase + -able _____

7. service + -able _____

8. service + -ing _____

9. peace + -ful _____

10. peace + -able _____

11. use + -ed _____

12. use + -able _____

Tax Return Forms

If you work, each January your employer will give you a *Wage and Tax Statement,* or W-2 form. (If you changed jobs during the year, or if you worked for more than one company, you will get a W-2 form from each employer.) You will also get a statement of payment from your bank or credit union if you have a savings account. You may also get a statement of payment from a company if you did a short-term job for them. Together, these statements tell you how much money you earned during the year. They also tell you how much money the government withheld for taxes. You might also have done jobs for which you did not get any kind of statement or record. You should have kept a list of all such earnings.

Once you have gotten your W-2 statements and statements of other earnings, you are ready to file an income tax return. Here are the steps for filing a tax return.

1. Choose the right tax return form.
2. Figure out your filing status and number of exemptions.
3. Figure out your taxable income.
4. Figure out the amount of tax that should be paid on your earnings.
5. Mail the completed tax form plus any money you may still owe in taxes to the government.

In this chapter you will learn about the first step: how to choose the tax return form that is right for you.

Which Tax Form?

There are three different tax return forms from which to choose. The three forms are 1040EZ, 1040A, and 1040. The tax return form you should use depends on four things:

1. Are you married or single?
2. Do you have any *dependents?* A dependent is a person who (a) lives in your home and (b) is supported by you.
3. How do you earn your money?
4. What *deductions* from your income will you claim? A deduction is a sum of money—a part of your earnings—on which you do not have to pay taxes. The more deductions you have, the less income tax you must pay.

The government prints a table to help you figure out which tax return you should file. Part of the table is shown on the right.

Look at the table. Column one deals with *filing status.* Your filing status can be single, married, or head of household. Only single people with no dependents can file 1040EZ. All others must use 1040A or 1040.

Column two deals with *exemptions.* You can subtract a certain amount of money from your income for each exemption you can claim. Everyone can claim himself or herself as an exemption. So everyone has at least one exemption. Exemptions can also be claimed for a spouse (husband or wife), for dependents, and for such conditions as blindness and old age. If you file form 1040EZ, you can claim only one exemption—yourself. If you want to claim other exemptions, you must file form 1040A or form 1040.

Column three deals with the way you earned your income. Suppose all your earnings came from a job and

	Filing status	Number of exemptions	Only income from	Itemized deductions
Form 1040EZ	Single only	Only one personal exemption for yourself	• Wages, salaries, tips • Interest of $400 or less	No itemized deductions (You may deduct part of some amounts you gave to charitable organizations)
Form 1040A	• Single • Married filing joint • Married filing separate • Head of household	All exemptions that you are entitled to claim	• Wages, salaries, tips • Interest • Dividends • Unemployment compensation	No itemized deductions (You may deduct part of some amounts you gave to charitable organizations)
Form 1040	• Single • Married filing joint • Married filing separate • Head of household • Qualifying widow(er) with dependent child	All exemptions that you are entitled to claim	• Wages, salaries, tips • Interest and dividends • Taxable social security and tier 1 railroad retirement benefits (see page 13) • Unemployment compensation • Self-employment compensation • Rents and royalties (Schedule E) • Pensions and annuities • Taxable state and local income tax refunds • Capital gains (Schedule D) • Gain from the sale of your home (Form 2119) • Alimony received • All other sources	All itemized deductions (Use Schedule A): • State and local income taxes • Real estate taxes • Sales taxes • Interest paid • Charitable contributions • Medical and dental expenses • Casualty and theft losses • Miscellaneous deductions

interest on a small savings account. Then you may use form 1040EZ. If you also got money from unemployment, you must use form 1040A or 1040. If you had special kinds of income, you have to file form 1040. Some special kinds of income are rents from buildings that you own, pensions after you have retired, earnings from your own business, and gains from the sale of a house.

Column four deals with *deductions*. You can subtract certain types of expenses from your income. These are called deductions. Some taxpayers *itemize,* or list, special deductions. Those taxpayers must use form 1040. Other people just take what is called the *standard deduction* that is given to every taxpayer. If you take the standard deduction, you can use form 1040EZ or form 1040A.

Choosing the Right Tax Form

You know that a taxpayer has three tax return forms from which to choose: 1040EZ, 1040A, and 1040. To choose the form that is right for you, you must first decide your filing status, number of exemptions, types of income, and kinds of deductions. You can then use the government table that will help you choose the form that is right for you.

Exercise

Which tax return form is right for each of the tax-payers in this exercise? Read the information about each person's filing status, exemptions, type of income and deductions. Then use the table on the next page to choose the right tax form for each taxpayer. Print 1040EZ, 1040A, or 1040 in the space provided. The first two have been done for you as examples.

1. Sara Green   Filing Status: single
                  Exemptions: one (no dependents)
                  Type of Income: pension
                  Deductions: none

    Sara Green should use form _____**1040**_____

2. Ronald Clark Filing Status: married
                  Exemptions: four (himself, a wife, and two children)
                  Type of Income: wages
                  Deductions: none

    Ronald Clark should use form _____**1040 A**_____

	Filing status	Number of exemptions	Only income from	Itemized deductions
Form 1040EZ	Single only	Only one personal exemption for yourself	• Wages, salaries, tips • Interest of $400 or less	No itemized deductions (You may deduct part of some amounts you gave to charitable organizations)
Form 1040A	• Single • Married filing joint • Married filing separate • Head of household	All exemptions that you are entitled to claim	• Wages, salaries, tips • Interest • Dividends • Unemployment compensation	No itemized deductions (You may deduct part of some amounts you gave to charitable organizations)
Form 1040	• Single • Married filing joint • Married filing separate • Head of household • Qualifying widow(er) with dependent child	All exemptions that you are entitled to claim	• Wages, salaries, tips • Interest and dividends • Taxable social security and tier 1 railroad retirement benefits (see page 13) • Unemployment compensation • Self-employment • Rents and royalties (Schedule E) • Pensions and annuities • Taxable state and local income tax refunds • Capital gains (Schedule D) • Gain from the sale of your home (Form 2119) • Alimony received • All other sources	All itemized deductions (Use Schedule A): • State and local income taxes • Real estate taxes • Sales taxes • Interest paid • Charitable contributions • Medical and dental expenses • Casualty and theft losses • Miscellaneous deductions

3. Alice Scott   Filing Status: single
Exemptions: two (one dependent)
Type of income: salary
Deductions: none

Alice Scott should use form _____

4. Peter Gill   Filing Status: single
Exemptions: one (no dependents)
Type of Income: wages, rents from an apartment building
Deductions: none

Peter Gill should use form _____

5. Nancy Peters   Filing Status: head of household
Exemptions: two (one child)
Type of Income: owns her own business
Deductions: itemized

Nancy Peters should use form _____

6. James Kent   Filing Status: single
Exemptions: one (no dependents)
Type of Income: salary
Deductions: none

James Kent should use form _____

7. Jane North   Filing Status: married
Exemptions: two (herself and her husband)
Type of Income: salary
Deductions: none

Jane North should use form _____

The Killer Strikes

Study the words in the box. Then read the sentences below with your teacher. Look carefully at the words in boldface type.

attack	enough	newspapers	Saturday
boring	finish	paperweight	screamed
breathe	follow	police	stolen
crashed	fuse	purple	taxi
detectives	knock	robbery	Tuesday

1. If anything is missing, old Clark will blow a **fuse**.
2. Shouldn't we **finish** up over here first?
3. "Of course you should finish up!" Clark **screamed**.
4. Clark stuck his **purple** face right into the supervisor's pale one.
5. Things have been **stolen** right out of the warehouse.
6. He makes me afraid to **breathe**.
7. I want you to **follow** three people who work for me.
8. I'll send over three **detectives** right away.
9. On **Saturday** afternoon, the detective reported about Sue.
10. "What a **boring** life!" Clark thought.
11. They weren't doing anything that would lead to a **robbery**.
12. Both robberies happened on **Tuesday** nights.
13. If the **newspapers** find out . . .
14. He hurried down to the street and called a **taxi**.
15. Lang was holding his big glass **paperweight**.
16. Just then there was a **knock** at the door.
17. Growing up with you was bad **enough**.
18. The paperweight **crashed** down on Clark's head.
19. The **police** might not understand that.
20. I will try to make them believe that he had a heart **attack**.

The next morning, bright and early, the sealed truck pulled out of the warehouse. But this time it was only going across the city. Soon the truck was pulling up to the house where it would be unloaded. The movers jumped out and walked around to the back of the truck. One man broke the seal and threw open the doors.

The things in the truck were all uncovered. The blankets were in a heap in the corner of the truck, where the two robbers had thrown them the night before. "Oh, oh, I don't like the looks of this!" one of the movers said.

"We'd better get this unloaded fast," said another, "so we can check the things off against our list. I sure hope nothing is missing!"

"Me, too! If anything *is* missing, old Clark will blow a fuse!"

They quickly unloaded the truck and checked their list. Yes, six small boxes were missing. The men flipped a coin to see who would call and tell Clark.

When Clark got the call, he jumped right out of his chair. "What!" he shouted. "The truck had been robbed? Again? Right here in my warehouse?"

"Well, yes, sir," said the mover on the other end of the line. "It looks that way, sir."

"Get back to the warehouse right away!" Clark shouted.

"Shouldn't we finish up over here first, sir? We've got to get everything into the house, and—"

"Of *course* you should finish up over there first!" Clark screamed. "You fool! You crazy, good-for-nothing—" Clark threw the phone against the wall.

At his end of the line, the mover hung up. He turned to

the other men and said, "I may never hear with this ear again."

Clark came roaring out of his office yelling, "Get me the supervisor! NOW!" The supervisor had heard him all the way out in the warehouse. He stuck his head into the main office and looked carefully around the corner. Clark spotted him and stuck his purple face right into the supervisor's pale one. "Get into my office!" he screamed. "And you'd better be ready to do some fast talking!"

As soon as they got into Clark's office, Clark said, "It's happened again! Things missing from a sealed truck! Things stolen right out of the warehouse, with no sign of anyone breaking in! Someone must be *letting* them in, and I want to know who!"

"Now see here, Mr. Clark," the supervisor started to say, "I don't think—"

"Shut up!" Clark shouted. "I don't want any back talk! Someone *is* in on this, and I'm going to find out who it is! Who has keys to the warehouse? And who can get at the truck seals?"

"Well, *I* have keys, of course," the supervisor said, "and the seals are kept in my office in the warehouse."

"OK, you have keys. Who else? Come on, who?"

"Well, Sue has a set of keys. And so does Omar. He's in charge of the loading dock. They are the only ones I can think of. And both Sue and Omar have been with us for years."

"All right," Clark said quickly, "change the locks. Give the new keys to Sue and Omar, but make sure no one else gets them."

"Yes, sir."

"Now get out of here!" Clark yelled. The supervisor opened the door and hurried out.

The people in the main office looked up as he came out. "The old man is at it again," a woman said.

"He sure is!" another woman said. "What a *grouch!* He gets mad every time something happens. He blames other people for everything. He makes me afraid to breathe!"

May Lee sat back in her chair and pushed back her long hair. "Well, just be glad you don't have to live with him!" she said.

"I couldn't stand it," the first woman said. "Think of his poor family! I just couldn't stand it."

In his office, Clark picked his phone up off the floor and called a company that he had heard about. "I need your help," he said, talking in a quiet voice for once. "There is something I have to find out. I want someone to follow three people who are working for me. I want to know everything about them, everything they do, and I want a report every day."

"All right," said a voice on the other end of the line,

"I'll send over three detectives right away."

The detectives were so good at their work that the three workers never knew that they were being followed. Every afternoon the detective phoned Clark to tell him what Sue, Omar, and the supervisor had done since the day before.

The first day, Sue left work, took a bus, and went to visit her father and stepmother, the detective reported. Then she went home and went to bed. She went to work again the next morning. After work the next day, and all the rest of the week, Sue just went home. She spent the evening watching TV, then went to bed early.

On Saturday afternoon, the detective reported that Sue had stayed home all day. On Sunday she went out only once, to visit her father and stepmother. "What a boring life!" Clark thought to himself.

The supervisor and Omar both got around more, the other detectives reported, but they didn't seem to be doing anything that would lead to a robbery.

"Keep on them," Clark told the detectives. "Both robberies happened on Tuesday nights, so I want you to watch them very carefully on Monday and Tuesday."

On Monday afternoon, the detective who was following Omar called up. "He left work and picked up his little girl," the detective said. "They took the bus across the city to a doctor's office. Then they went home again. Right now he is having supper with his family."

"OK, OK," Clark said. He hung up the phone, then sat with his face in his hands. The detectives weren't getting anywhere. But they had to find out! If there was another robbery, it would be sometime tomorrow night. And if the newspapers found out, it would be the end of his company. He sat and stared glumly at the phone, waiting for the other detectives to make their reports.

The phone rang again. "Last night, after she visited her father, Sue went right home and—" the detective started to say.

"I know, I know," Clark cut in, "she went home and went to bed. She never does anything new."

"Well, today she did do something new," the detective said. "She went to see a hypnotist. She's there right now."

"A hypnotist?" Clark asked quickly. "Did you say she's seeing a hypnotist? What's his name?"

"His name is Lorenzo Lang," the detective said.

"Lorenzo Lang . . ." Clark said to himself. Thoughts began to race through his head. "I wonder," he thought, "is that what he's calling himself these days? I hadn't heard that he was back in the city. But that could be it! If anyone could get a good worker to rob her boss, *he* could."

"Mr. Clark, are you there?" the detective asked.

"Yes, I'm here," Clark told the detective. "I think we may have something here. You say that she's with Lang right now?"

"Yes, she just went in."

"Quick, what's the address?" The detective gave Clark the address. "Good work. This may be it. I'll call you tomorrow if I need you anymore," Clark told the detective.

"Yes, sir."

"Thank you," Clark said, and hung up the phone. Then he jumped up and ran out of the office. He hurried out to the street and called a taxi. He gave Lang's address to the driver and said, "Hurry!"

"It's not far," the driver said as he pulled out.

A few minutes later, the taxi pulled up in front of Lang's building. Clark jumped out and hurried into the building.

Upstairs, Lang had just hypnotized Sue. She sat

quietly with her eyes closed. Her breathing was slow and quiet. Lang was sitting at his desk, holding his big glass paperweight in his hands and smiling to himself. "One more robbery should do it," he said to himself, turning the paperweight over and over in his hands. "Then people will begin to talk—"

Just then, there was a knock at the door. Lang got up and opened the door a little way, saying, "What is it? I—"

Clark threw the door open all the way, stepped into the office, and slammed the door shut. "You!" he shouted at Lang. "I should have known it would be you!"

"Robert! What are you doing here?" Lang asked. He tried to calm himself, adding, "What a nice surprise. It's very good of you to come to see me like this." As he spoke, Lang started to move quietly toward the door.

"Oh no you don't!" Clark yelled, grabbing Lang by the front of his shirt. "You aren't going anywhere! You're staying right here and telling me what you're doing with my workers! Where is she?"

"Where is who?" Lang asked.

"She must be here somewhere," Clark said, dragging Lang into the other room. When he saw Sue sitting there, he stopped short. "Sue, what are you doing here?" he asked.

Sue did not move.

Clark grabbed Lang harder. "What have you done to her?" he yelled. His face was getting red.

"She is hypnotized," Lang said in a thin voice. "I *am* a hypnotist, you know. I am helping her to get rid of her headaches. *You* give her those. You and your yelling and shouting. You—"

"Shut up!" Clark shouted. "You can't talk to me like

that! I won't let you! No baby brother of mine is going to talk to me like that!"

"Don't call me your baby brother!" Lang shouted. "I don't want to think about being your brother. Growing up with you was bad enough! All the shouting! The way you beat us up . . . you even hit our mother! The way you made us all afraid of you. You made a mess of our lives. But that's all over now. I'll never be afraid of you again. And everything you do, I'll find some way to mess it up!"

"So you did do it!" Clark shouted. He pointed at Sue.

"You got her to give you her keys!" He let go of Lang and ran over to Sue. "I'll get you for that!" he shouted at her. "I'll—"

"She can't hear you, Robert," Lang said. "She can't hear anything unless I tell her to. She's not your worker anymore. She's mine."

"Why, you—" Clark turned to Lang again. He raised his hands to grab him by the coat again, but Lang ran out into his office. "I'll get you for this!" Clark yelled, running after him. He reached out for Lang. Lang looked wildly around him, grabbed the glass paperweight, and raised it high. The heavy paperweight crashed down on Clark's head. Clark fell to the floor and lay still.

Lang dropped the paperweight. He stood looking down at Clark and waited.

Clark didn't move.

Suddenly Lang dropped to the floor and turned Clark over. He put his hand down on Clark's chest. Then he sat back and looked down at his brother. "He's dead!" Lang said softly. "I can't believe it! He's dead!"

Lang stood up and walked around the room. He walked around and around the chair where Sue was sitting, asleep. "What am I going to do?" he asked himself. "How can I get rid of his body? The police will find it. They'll see his head . . . They'll start asking questions and they'll find out how much I hated him." He stopped short and looked at Sue. "And she'll tell them she was here! Then they'll find out about the robberies. They'll find out everything!"

He walked slowly around Sue. "What shall I do with her?" he asked himself. "I can't tell her to forget that she was here, because that other girl, May Lee, would know that something was up." He stopped and looked hard at

Sue, who just sat there quietly, her eyes closed. "Maybe I should kill her too."

He walked over and looked out the window. "I could kill her, and then . . . No, that would just make things worse. Wait, I know!" He turned around quickly. "I've got it! I'll tell her that she did it! She might even turn herself in!"

Lang stopped to think about what he was going to say to Sue. Then he turned to her and asked, "Can you hear me?"

"Yes," Sue said.

"Stand up and come over here." He took Sue by the hand and led her out into the office, to Clark's body. Then he put the paperweight into her hands. "When I count to five, you will wake up," he told her. "You will remember nothing of what has gone on here. You will believe what I am going to tell you. Do you understand?"

"Yes," Sue said.

"OK," Lang said, "one . . . two . . . three . . . four . . . five!"

Sue opened her eyes. She looked around the room, then down at the paperweight she was holding. Then she saw Clark's body. "Mr. Clark! What . . . what happened to him?" she asked in a dazed voice.

"Sue, something very bad has happened. You cannot know how bad I feel about this," Lang said sadly.

"But what happened?"

"You were hypnotized. You were in a deep trance. We were trying to find out more about your headaches. You were telling me about how much you hated Mr. Clark. You did hate him very much, didn't you?"

"Yes, but . . ."

"And then Clark broke in here," Lang said. "He must

have followed you—I don't know why. But when you saw him, you ran out here and grabbed that paperweight. You were so quick that I couldn't stop you. You picked it up and hit him over the head."

Sue looked down at the paperweight in her hands. "I hit him?"

"Yes. You hit him, and he's dead.

"Dead! Oh, no!" Sue cried, dropping the paperweight. It hit the floor with a heavy thud.

"Yes, I'm afraid so," Lang said, walking over to Sue and putting his arm around her. He led her back to the desk and helped her to sit down in a chair. "People can do strange things when they are in a deep trance," he told her. "Nothing like this ever happened before when I hypnotized someone, and I will make sure that it never happens again. I will never hypnotize anyone again. Never."

"Oh, Mr. Lang," Sue said. She stared at Clark's body, lying still on the floor.

"You must not blame yourself, my dear," Lang said softly. "You were not in your right mind when it happened. But the police might not understand that."

"The police!"

"Well, my dear, I do have to call the police. I will have to tell them why there is a dead body on the floor of my office. But I will not tell them that you were here. I will try to make them believe that he had a heart attack."

"But . . ."

"I will tell them that he had a sudden heart attack and just fell over onto the floor. I will tell them that he hit his head on the desk as he fell. Let me see . . ." He bent down and took hold of Clark's body under the arms. "I will move him over closer to the desk," he said, dragging the body across the floor. "There, that should do it."

He stood up and looked at Sue. "Do not worry," he told her. "I think the police will believe me. After all, everyone knew how mad Clark could get. He would have had a heart attack one of these days." Sue just sat there, staring at the body by the desk. "You go home now," Lang said.

"Try to forget that this ever happened. Try to put it out of your mind. Remember what I have shown you about how to relax, and try to be calm." He led Sue to the door. "Good-bye. I am very sorry that this happened. I will always be sorry that I could not stop you in time. But I will do my best to help you now. Do not worry, I will take care of everything."

"Oh, thank you, Mr. Lang."

"Good-bye."

Sue walked out of Lang's office. She walked slowly down the hall and pushed the button for the elevator. Then she leaned against the wall and started to cry.

Directions. Answer these questions about the chapter you have just read. Put an *x* in the box beside the best answer to each question.

1. (D) Why did the movers flip a coin to see who would tell Clark about the robbery?

   ☐ a. They knew that Clark would yell when he found out.
   ☐ b. They all wanted to be the one to call him.
   ☐ c. They all wanted to win the coin.
   ☐ d. They didn't want to do any more work that day.

2. (C) When the movers told Clark that another truck had been robbed, what was the first thing he did?

   ☐ a. He called the supervisor.
   ☐ b. He called the detectives.
   ☐ c. He threw the phone against the wall.
   ☐ d. He followed Sue to Lang's office.

3. (B) Who had keys to the supervisor's office?

   ☐ a. Everyone who worked on the loading dock
   ☐ b. The supervisor, Sue and Omar
   ☐ c. Sue and May Lee
   ☐ d. No one but Clark and the supervisor

4. (B) How did Clark know that Sue went to visit her father?

☐ a. The detective told him.
☐ b. Clark followed her.
☐ c. Sue's father told him.
☐ d. Clark asked May Lee.

5. (D) Why did Clark go to Lang's office?

☐ a. He wanted to be hypnotized too.
☐ b. He knew that the hypnotist might be his brother.
☐ c. He wanted to tell Sue not to get hypnotized.
☐ d. He was going to call the police.

6. (E) What was the main reason that Lang hated Clark?

☐ a. Clark's Moving and Storage had lost all his silver.
☐ b. Clark had made a mess of Lang's show.
☐ c. Clark yelled at Sue and gave her headaches.
☐ d. Clark was mean to him when they were boys.

7. (E) What was the main thing that happened in this part of the story?

☐ a. Another truck was robbed.
☐ b. Sue went to visit her father.
☐ c. Lang killed Clark.
☐ d. Lang hypnotized Sue.

8. (A) Lang said, "I'll tell Sue that she killed Clark. She might even *turn herself in!*" What did he mean?

☐ a. She would go and tell the police that she did it.

☐ b. She would turn around and around till she got dizzy.

☐ c. She would change her mind about Clark.

☐ d. She would turn around and go inside the building.

9. (C) What was the last thing Lang did just before he told Sue to wake up?

☐ a. He killed Clark.

☐ b. He told Sue that she had killed Clark.

☐ c. He called the police.

☐ d. He put the paperweight in Sue's hands.

10. (A) Lang told Sue, "You were *not in your right mind* when it happened." What does that mean?

☐ a. She thought she was May Lee.

☐ b. Sue was not in control of her thoughts.

☐ c. Sue didn't mind talking to him.

☐ d. Sue had no right to do it.

Skills Used to Answer Questions
A. Recognizing Words in Context   B. Recalling Facts
C. Keeping Events in Order   D. Making Inferences
E. Understanding Main Ideas

Double Consonants: Part One

You have learned that when you add a suffix to a root word to form a new word, you must sometimes change the spelling of the root. You know when and how to change the spelling of roots that end in the letter *e*. Now you will learn when and how to change the spelling of roots that end in consonants. Look at the roots, suffixes and new words below.

spot + -ed = spotted

fun + -y = funny

Both roots are words of only one syllable. A syllable is a word or a part of a word that is said as one sound. For instance, *spot* is said in one sound, while *spotted* is two sounds. A syllable is usually made up of a vowel alone or of a vowel together with one or more consonants.

Both the word *spot* and the word *fun* end with *one vowel and one consonant.* Spot ends in *ot,* and fun ends in *un.*

The suffix *-ed* begins with a vowel, and the suffix *-y* is a vowel. (It has an *e* sound.)

To put the roots and the suffixes together to make new words, a spelling change is needed. The final consonants of the roots must be doubled. The word *spotted* has two *t*'s, and the word *funny* has two *n*'s.

The rule for this spelling change is: if the root ends in a single vowel and a single consonant, and the suffix begins with a vowel, the final consonant of the root must be doubled before adding the suffix.

Now look at these roots, suffixes and new words:

$$man + \text{-ly} = manly$$
$$stoop + \text{-ed} = stooped$$
$$want + \text{-ing} = wanting$$

Notice that there is no spelling change in the new words made by putting those roots and suffixes together. The word *man* is a word of one syllable that ends in a single vowel and a single consonant, but the suffix *-ly* begins with a consonant. That is why the *n* at the end of *man* is not doubled.

In the second example, the suffix *-ed* does begin with a vowel, but the root *stoop* does not end in a single vowel and a single consonant. It ends with the double vowel *oo* and the single consonant *p*. So the final *p* in *stoop* is not doubled to make *stooped*.

In the third example, the suffix *-ing* begins with a vowel and the root is a word of one syllable. But *want* ends with two consonants, *nt*. So the *t* at the end of *want* is not doubled to make the word *wanted*.

Spelling Rule #3: When adding a suffix to a one-syllable root word that ends in a consonant, double the final consonant if
    (a) the root ends in a single vowel and a single consonant, and
    (b) the suffix begins with a vowel.

Exercise 1

Below is a list of roots and suffixes. All the roots are words of one syllable. They all end in a single vowel and a single consonant. All the suffixes begin with a vowel. Add the suffixes to the roots to make new words. Remember to double the final consonant of each root before adding the suffix. Print the new word on the line provided. The first one has been done for you as an example.

1. red + -en _____*redden*_____

2. cut + -er _____

3. pat + -ed _____

4. stop + -ing _____

5. hog + -ish _____

6. spot + -y _____

Exercise 2

Below is a list of roots and suffixes. All the roots are one-syllable words. They all end in a single vowel and a single consonant. Some of the suffixes begin with a vowel, others begin with a consonant. Add the suffixes to the roots to make new words. Remember to double the final consonant if the suffix begins with a vowel. Do not double it if the suffix begins with a consonant. Print the new word on the line provided. The first two have been done for you.

1. dim + -ly   *dimly*

2. dim + -ed   *dimmed*

3. cup + -ful _____

4. bit + -en _____

5. sap + -y _____

6. plan + -er _____

7. fat + -en _____

8. fat + -ness _____

9. red + -ish _____

10. hat + -less _____

Exercise 3

Make new words from the roots and suffixes below. All the suffixes begin with vowels. Some of the roots end in a single vowel and a single consonant. Some end in two consonants. Some end with two vowels and one consonant. To make the new words, follow these steps:

1. Check the spelling of the root word. If it ends in a single vowel and a single consonant, print *VC* in the box next to it. If it ends in two consonants, print *CC* in the box next to it. If it ends with a double vowel and a single consonant, print *VVC*.

2. Add the suffix to the root. Make no spelling change if you have printed *VVC* or *CC* in the box. Double the final consonant of the root if you have printed *VC* in the box.

3. Print the new word on the line provided.

The first two have been done for you as examples.

1. read |VVC| read + -er *reader* _____

2. rot |VC| rot + -en *rotten* _____

3. end | | end + -ing _____

4. sun | | sun + -y _____

5. hoot | | hoot + -ing _____

6. cup | | cup + -ed _____

7. thin | | thin + -er _____

8. wind | | wind + -ing _____

9. hid ☐ hid + -en _____

10. run ☐ run + -er _____

Filing Status and Exemptions

You know that you must take five steps to file an income tax return. You must:

1. choose the right tax form
2. figure out your filing status and number of exemptions
3. figure out your taxable income
4. figure out how much tax you must pay on your earnings
5. mail the completed tax form plus any money you may still owe in taxes to the government

You know how to go about choosing the right tax form. Now you will learn how to figure your filing status and exemptions.

Deciding on Your Filing Status

The filing status section of a tax form is shown below.

Step 2 Check your filing status (Check only one)	1 □ Single.
	2 □ Married filing joint return.
	3 □ Married filing separate return.
	4 □ Head of household.

You can see that there are four possible filing statuses:

1. Single
2. Married filing joint return
3. Married filing separate return
4. Head of household

Your filing status is *single* if you are not married and have no dependents. (Remember that a dependent is someone who lives in your house and is supported by you.

Dependents may be your children, your parents, or your brothers and sisters.)

Married people can file separate returns, or they may file a joint return.

A joint return is one tax form that shows the income of both the husband and the wife. The amount of tax that the couple must pay is figured on their combined earnings. A couple filing on one form would choose the status *Married filing joint return.*

If a married couple wishes to file separate tax returns, each person would choose the status *Married filing separate return.*

The filing status *Head of household* is for single people who have dependents.

Exemptions

An exemption allows you to subtract a certain amount of money from your income. That means that you do not have to pay taxes on that amount. The more exemptions you have, the less tax you must pay.

As a taxpayer, you know that you can claim at least one exemption—for yourself. But you may also be able to claim other exemptions. The possible exemptions that a person can claim are listed on the tax form on the next page. It has been filled in by a taxpayer. The form tells you that you may claim one exemption for each of the following:

1. for yourself
2. for your spouse if you are married
3. if you are over the age of 65
4. if you have a spouse over the age of 65
5. if you are blind
6. if you have a spouse who is blind
7. for each dependent

Step 3 Figure your exemptions	Always check the exemption box labeled Yourself. Check other boxes if they apply.			
	5a ☒ Yourself ☐ 65 or over ☐ Blind		Write number of boxes checked on 5a and b	2
	b ☒ Spouse ☐ 65 or over ☐ Blind			
	c First names of your dependent children who lived with you			
	Luis Donna		Write number of children listed on 5c	+2
	d Other dependents:			
	1. Name	2. Relationship		
	Tony Romero	father	Write number of other dependents listed on 5d	+1
	e Total number of exemptions claimed.		Add numbers entered on lines above	=5

To complete the exemptions sections of a tax return, follow these steps:

1. Put a check mark in the box marked *Yourself*.
2. Check any other boxes that apply to you. (The taxpayer in the sample checked the box marked *Spouse*.)
3. In the space provided to the right of the exemption boxes that you checked, write the number of boxes checked. (The sample taxpayer entered the number 2, for herself and her spouse.)
4. Print the names of your dependent children in space 5c. In the box to the right, fill in the number of children you are claiming. (The sample taxpayer wrote 2, for her children Luis and Donna.)
5. Print the names of other dependents on line 5d. In the box to the right, fill in the number of other dependents you are claiming. (The sample taxpayer supports her father, whose name is Tony Romero.)
6. Add the numbers you entered in the boxes on the right side of the form. Write that number on the bottom line. (This taxpayer has a total of 5 exemptions.)

Figuring Filing Status and Exemptions

You know that there are four possible tax filing statuses: single, married filing joint return, married filing separate return, and head of household.

You also know that taxpayers can claim exemptions for themselves, their spouses and their dependents. They can also claim exemptions if they or their spouses are over 65, or if they or their spouses are blind. On a tax return, a taxpayer should check off all the exemptions that he or she is allowed.

Exercise 1

Read about each of the taxpayers described below. How many exemptions can each of them claim? Circle the number of exemptions that each taxpayer can claim. The first one has been done for you as an example.

1. Ralph Barton is forty-five years old. His wife is forty-seven. The couple has two grown children. The children do not live at home. How many exemptions can Ralph Barton claim?

    1   (2)   3   4

2. Maria Kenmore is sixty-three years old. Her husband is sixty-six. He is blind. They have no children. How many exemptions can Maria Kenmore claim?

    1   2   3   4

3. Jack Sales is sixty-eight years old. He is single with no dependents. How many exemptions can he claim?

        1   2   3   4

4. Jennifer Bailey is twenty-seven years old. Her husband is thirty. They have two small children. How many exemptions can Jennifer Bailey claim?

        1   2   3   4

5. Sara Richards is forty-five years old. She supports her sick brother who lives in her home. How many exemptions can Sara Richards claim?

        1   2   3   4

Exercise 2

Suppose you are a married taxpayer. You and your spouse want to file on one tax return. You have two children, named Jane and Donald, living at home. You have no other dependents. You are claiming a total of four exemptions.

Use this information to enter your filing status and exemptions on the tax form on the right. Follow these steps:

1. Check the box next to the filing status you want.
2. Check the exemption box marked *Yourself,* and all other exemption boxes that apply to you.
3. Write the names of your dependent children on the line provided.
4. In the spaces provided on the right side of the form, write the number of exemptions that you are claiming.

The total number of exemptions you can claim is four. The number 4 has already been entered on the form for you.

Step 2
Check your filing status
(Check only one)

1. ☐ Single.
2. ☐ Married filing joint return.
3. ☐ Married filing separate return.
4. ☐ Head of household.

Step 3
Figure your exemptions

Always check the exemption box labeled Yourself. Check other boxes if they apply.

5a ☐ Yourself ☐ 65 or over ☐ Blind

b ☐ Spouse ☐ 65 or over ☐ Blind
      Write number of boxes checked on 5a and b

c First names of your dependent children who lived with you
      Write number of children listed on 5c

d Other dependents:

1. Name	2. Relationship

Write number of other dependents listed on 5d

Attach Copy B of Form(s) W-2 here

e Total number of exemptions claimed.
      Add numbers entered on lines above = 4

5

To End
It All

Study the words in the box. Then read the sentences below with your teacher. Look carefully at the words in boldface type.

anyway	encyclopedia	library	shaking
backward	excited	money	slumped
death	headed	murderer	stringing
died	hey	please	true
empty	hypnotism	questioning	yesterday

1. May Lee sounded very **excited**.
2. Even May Lee wouldn't want to be the friend of a **murderer**.
3. Mr. Clark **died** last night.
4. Well it's **true**, and you know it.
5. Her voice was **shaking**.
6. You were there **yesterday** too, weren't you?
7. "**Hey**, Sue, it's me!" May Lee's voice called.
8. "Oh no, **please** don't," Sue said.
9. But May Lee went right on **anyway**.
10. There's something strange about Mr. Clark's **death**.
11. Mr. Lang has been called in for **questioning**.
12. Sue **slumped** down in her chair.
13. She took a step **backward**.
14. We can look it up in the **encyclopedia**.
15. Let's go over to the **library**.
16. They got on the bus and **headed** downtown.
17. May Lee pulled down the H book for **Hypnotism**.
18. Her voice sounded flat and **empty**.
19. That's a lot of **money**.
20. He must have been **stringing** you along.

When Sue got home that night, she went right to bed, but she couldn't sleep. She just lay staring into the dark, thinking—thinking about Clark's body, lying so still on the floor of Lang's office. Thinking about what she had done.

In the morning she did not go to work at Clark's Moving and Storage. She knew that she would never go back to work there. Maybe she would never go to work anywhere, ever again.

She just sat in her apartment and looked out the window, watching people go by in the street. They looked so happy walking along. She would never be happy again. She felt so sad and so alone.

In the middle of the morning the phone rang. She jumped up and stood looking at the phone. Should she pick it up? It might be the police!

The phone rang and rang. At last Sue reached out her hand to the phone. She let it ring one more time, then picked it up. She opened her mouth, but her voice seemed to be stuck. At last she croaked out, "Hello?"

"Sue, is that you? Are you all right?" It was May Lee, and she sounded very excited.

"Oh, May Lee!" Sue said, so happy to hear a friendly voice that she almost cried.

"I'm sorry, Sue," May Lee said. "I must have woken you up. Are you having a bad headache today? I shouldn't have called you, but I have some news to tell you! I could hardly wait until the break to call you!"

Sue didn't say anything. She just listened to May Lee's voice. It felt so good to have a friend! But what if May Lee found out what Sue had done? Even May Lee wouldn't want to be the friend of a murderer!

"Sue, are you still there?" May Lee was asking. "Don't you want to hear my news? Mr. Clark is dead! He died last night. What do you think of that?"

Sue couldn't say anything at all.

After a moment, May Lee went on, "Everyone is so surprised. Aren't you surprised? They think he had a heart attack. The old grouch must have gotten mad one last time."

"May Lee, don't talk like that!" Sue burst out.

"Well it's true, and you know it. But that's not all the news. I haven't told you the most surprising part yet! Where do you think he died?"

"I don't know. Where?" Sue asked in a shaking voice.

"In Lorenzo Lang's office! Your hypnotist! *Now* are you surprised?"

Sue's voice came out very small and far away. "Yes," was all she could say.

"It was in the newspaper this morning," May Lee

said. "Mr. Lang said that Mr. Clark went to be hypnotized late last night. You were there yesterday too, weren't you? But earlier. Anyway, Mr. Clark got there later, and then he had a heart attack—right there in Mr. Lang's office! Do you want me to bring you the newspaper? At lunch time they're going to close the company for the rest of the day."

"No—no thank you," Sue said quickly.

"Don't you want to read all about it?" May Lee asked.

"No, I don't. I've got to go now, May Lee. I've got to go back to bed. Good-bye." Sue hung up the phone.

How was she going to stand it?

Time passed slowly. Sue just sat and looked out the window.

Maybe she should go to the police and tell them everything, just as Lang had told her it had happened. But then she would go to jail for murder. If only she could talk to someone about it. If only someone could help her think what to do.

She got up and walked around her apartment. She tried to eat some lunch, but she couldn't get the food down. Slowly the day went by. Then, just as it was beginning to get dark, there was a knock on the door.

Sue jumped up from her chair and stood staring at the door. She couldn't move. Was it the police? Were they coming for her?

Knock! Knock! It came again. Sue didn't move, but at last she called softly, "Who is it?"

"Hey, Sue, it's me!" May Lee's voice called. "Can I come in?"

Sue moved slowly toward the door on stiff, heavy legs. She slowly opened the door.

May Lee walked quickly into the apartment and closed the door. She took Sue by both arms and said,

"Sue, what's the matter? I've never seen you look so bad! What's the matter with you? I got to thinking about you, and I thought I'd better come over. I'm glad I did." She led Sue carefully over to a chair and made her sit down. "Can I get you anything?" she asked.

"No, I'm all right," Sue said.

"No, you're not," May Lee said. "The headaches must be getting worse. And I thought Mr. Lang was really helping you. Well I've got some more news for you. This will help you get your mind off your headache." She pulled out an evening newspaper. "Wait until you hear the latest about Mr. Clark and Mr. Lang!"

"Oh no, please don't," Sue cried.

But May Lee went right on. "The newspaper says that there's something strange about Mr. Clark's death. First Mr. Lang said that Mr. Clark had had a heart attack. But there was a lump on his head. Well, Lang said that Clark hit his head as he fell, but the police said there was no sign of a heart attack. It was the blow to his head that killed him. Also, they could tell that Clark had been moved after he died!"

"Oh," Sue said. She felt as if she was going to be sick.

"That's not all! Mr. Lang said that Mr. Clark died about nine o'clock. But the police think he died earlier than that," May Lee said, looking at the newspaper. "They think he died at about six! Anyway, Mr. Lang has been called in for questioning."

"He has? Oh, no!" Sue gasped, then slumped down in her chair. It was all over then.

"Sue, what's the matter?" May Lee asked as she ran to Sue and put her arms around her. "What's the matter? You can tell me—you have to tell me!"

Sue leaned her head against May Lee's arm. Suddenly she started to cry. She cried and cried, as May Lee patted her softly. At last, when she could talk, Sue said,

"I might as well tell you—you'll be reading it in the newspaper anyway."

"Reading about what?" May Lee asked.

"May Lee, Mr. Clark didn't have a heart attack. I killed him."

"*What?* You . . . you killed him?" May Lee stood up quickly and took a step backward. "Sue, you couldn't do a thing like that! No matter how much you hated him, you couldn't . . . you couldn't *kill* him!"

"But I did! Mr. Lang said so!"

"Mr. Lang said so? Sue, tell me about it," May Lee said as she sat down on the floor in front of Sue and lit a cigarette with shaking hands.

Sue took a deep breath, then told May Lee all about the night before at Lang's office. "So Mr. Lang said that he'd try to save me," Sue said as she finished the story, "but it looks as if it didn't work. If Mr. Lang has been called in for questioning, I should turn myself in—before they come for me!" Sue started to cry again.

May Lee sat still, deep in thought. Then she said, "Wait a minute. How do you *know* you killed Mr. Clark? Do you remember doing it?"

"No, of course not! I told you—I was hypnotized!"

"Then how do you know it's true? How do you know Mr. Lang didn't do it?" May Lee asked.

"Oh, May Lee, Mr. Lang wouldn't do a thing like that!"

"But, Sue, that's just it! *You* wouldn't do a thing like that!" May Lee said. "And I know you a lot better than we know Mr. Lang. You couldn't have done it!"

"But I was hypnotized!"

"That's what I mean! I've heard that a person won't do something when hypnotized that he wouldn't do while awake."

"Really? Are you sure?"

"Yes, I'm sure. If you don't believe me, we can look it up. I know! Let's go over to the library and look it up in the encyclopedia."

"OK!" Sue said, and she jumped up. Suddenly everything went black for a moment. Sue grabbed for the back of her chair and held on until she could see again.

May Lee looked hard at her. "Sue," she asked, "when is the last time you ate?"

"I don't know," Sue said.

"OK, we eat supper first, then we go over to the library. I'm hungry anyway," May Lee added as she hurried into the kitchen. Soon they were eating supper. Sue had never been so hungry. And it felt so good to have a friend!

As soon as they were finished eating, they put on their coats and hurried out the door. They got to the street just as the bus did. They got on the bus and headed downtown feeling happy and excited.

But when they got to the library, all at once Sue began to feel afraid again. What if . . . ? She held back, but May Lee pulled her up the library steps, saying, "Come on. I'm right, you'll see!"

They walked across the quiet room to the encyclopedia. May Lee pulled down the H book and flipped through the pages. "Here it is—Hypnotism." She started to read quickly, but suddenly she stopped and gasped, "Oh, no!"

"What? What is it?" Sue asked. May Lee tried to close the book, but Sue grabbed it away from her and read from the page that May Lee had been looking at. "People used to think that a person would not do anything while hypnotized that he would not do while awake," she read. "People used to think that a hypnotized person could not hurt anyone. But it has been shown that this is not true. A hypnotized person *can* be made to hurt people."

The big book dropped from Sue's hands. "Oh, no!" she groaned. Some people sitting near them looked up from their books. May Lee tried to get Sue to be quiet, but Sue put her head in her hands and groaned again, even more loudly.

"Sue, Sue, it's all right!" May Lee said. "The book just said that it *could* happen. That doesn't mean that it *did* happen. Sue, it's all right!" She patted Sue's head and tried to get her to sit up.

Sue picked up the encyclopedia book and read the page again. "A hypnotized person *can* be made to hurt someone . . . Oh, I can't stand it! I can't . . . Oh, what am I going to do?"

May Lee looked around quickly. Everyone in the library was staring at them. They had to get out of there! May Lee grabbed Sue and pulled her out of her chair. She slammed the H book back into its place, then pulled Sue across the room and out the front door. The door closed behind them, but May Lee could still feel the eyes looking at them. She pulled Sue quickly down the sidewalk, away from the library.

Not until they had turned the corner and were out of sight of the library did May Lee let go of Sue. She leaned against the side of a building and looked at Sue. Sue was standing still. She had not moved since May Lee had let go of her. She was staring straight ahead, as if she had been hypnotized again. Her mouth moved as if she were talking, but no sound came out.

"Sue," May Lee said, "what are you saying? What are you going to do?"

Sue didn't move. She just stared straight ahead without seeing anything. When she started to talk again, May Lee could hardly hear what she was saying. "I can't stand it," Sue said in a flat, empty voice. "I can't stand it any more. There's only one way. I'm going to end it all."

"Sue, no!" May Lee grabbed Sue and shook her. "No, you can't kill yourself! You can't let him get you like this! You've got to fight him!" She shook Sue harder. "Sue, snap out of it! Sue!"

May Lee let go of Sue. Sue stood still for a moment, then turned to look at May Lee. She looked as if she were just waking up from a long sleep. "What am I going to do?" she asked quietly."

"You can . . . We can . . . We should . . ." May Lee stopped. What *should* they do? At last she said, "I don't know."

They stood quietly, thinking. Then Sue said, "Maybe I should go back to Lang's office."

"Oh, Sue, don't go back to see Lang again! He—"

"No, no, I don't mean that. I'm not going to go see Lang. I'm going to go to his office. I'm going to break in. Maybe I could find something that would tell me what happened—one way or the other."

"Oh, you couldn't—" May Lee started to say. Then she said, "Wait, I just thought of something! Remember that first time you went to see Lang? I was with you, and I remember that he had a little notebook on his desk. I saw him take some notes when you talked to him."

"Really? Maybe he took notes every time I was there. Maybe the notes would tell me something. I'm going to try it."

"And I'm going with you," May Lee said.

"No, you can't! What if—"

"Yes, I am. I'm going with you." May Lee grabbed Sue's arm and pulled her along the street. "Come on— before I think about *what if!*"

They took a bus to Lang's office. They got off the bus a block away, then walked slowly down the other side of the street and stopped across from Lang's office building.

The windows of Lang's office were dark.

"He's not there," Sue said. "Come on."

They crossed the street and went in the front door of the building. They got into the elevator, and Sue pushed the button. The elevator moved up and stopped at the floor where Lang's office was. The door opened.

Sue and May Lee did not move.

The doors closed.

The elevator stayed where it was. Sue and May Lee looked at each other for a long moment. Then Sue pushed the button to open the elevator doors again, and they stepped out and quietly walked down the hall to Lang's office.

The door was locked. "Let's try this," May Lee said, taking a card out of her pocketbook. She pushed it into the door frame, against the lock. "We're in luck! It's going to work!" she said, as the lock slipped back.

They opened the door and stepped into the office. May Lee stood by the door and told Sue, "I'll watch, in case he comes back."

"OK," Sue said, as she walked quickly over to the desk and pulled it open. She went through the papers until she found the hypnotist's notebook. She held it so she could see it by the light from the hall, and started to look at the pages.

"Did you find it?" May Lee asked. "What does it say?"

"He hasn't put anything into it for the last few days. There's nothing since I . . . There's nothing since Mr. Clark was killed."

"Oh. Well let's go, OK?"

"Wait a minute, I want to see if there's anything about me. Let's see . . . When was the first time I came here? Oh, here it is."

"What did he say about you?" May Lee asked.

"He just wrote down my name. Then it says *headaches* and *hard to get into deep trance.* I wish I never had got into a deep trance! Then it says *forty dollars—maybe sixty dollars.* What do you think that means?"

"It sounds as if he wanted to make you pay even more," May Lee said. "That's a lot of money."

Sue turned some more pages. "Let's look at the next week. Hey, look at this!"

"What?" May Lee asked, hurrying over to the desk.

"It says *deep trance,* then it says something about my father. I can't read all of it."

"Let me try," May Lee said. "It says *Father lost job*

when she was three years old. Mother left. Sue is afraid that no one will love her if she loses her job. Gives her headaches."

"What?" Sue gasped, grabbing for the notebook. "He never told me that! He said that he hadn't found out anything yet!"

"He must have been stringing you along, Sue!" May Lee said. "He must have wanted you to keep coming back. That means—"

Just then they heard a sound out in the hall. The elevator doors were opening. Someone was getting out. It was Lang.

Directions. Answer these questions about the chapter you have just read. Put an *x* in the box beside the best answer to each question.

1. (B) When Sue heard a knock on her door, who did she think it was at first?

    ☐ a. The police
    ☐ b. Clark
    ☐ c. Lang
    ☐ d. May Lee

2. (D) May Lee had a newspaper that told all about Clark's death. Why didn't Sue want to read it?

    ☐ a. She felt terrible about Clark's death because she thought she had killed him.
    ☐ b. She felt bad about Clark's death because she had liked Clark so much.
    ☐ c. She had already read all about it.
    ☐ d. She didn't like to read the newspaper.

3. (A) May Lee told Sue that Lang had been *called in for questioning*. What does that mean?

    ☐ a. Lang had hypnotized May Lee and asked her some questions.
    ☐ b. The police had told Lang that they wanted to ask him some questions.
    ☐ c. The police had told Lang that he would have to go to jail.
    ☐ d. Lang had asked Sue what she thought of Clark.

4. (E) May Lee didn't think that Sue had killed Clark. What was the main reason she felt that way?

☐ a. Lang had told her that he did it.
☐ b. She didn't think that Sue had been hypnotized.
☐ c. She knew that Sue would never do such a thing.
☐ d. She knew that Sue had not gone to Lang's office.

5. (E) What was the main thing that May Lee did for Sue in this part of the story?

☐ a. She got supper for Sue.
☐ b. She read Sue the newspaper.
☐ c. She showed Sue how to get to Lang's office.
☐ d. She showed that she was Sue's friend.

6. (B) Why did Sue and May Lee go to the library?

☐ a. To take back some books
☐ b. To find out more about hypnotism
☐ c. To hide from the police
☐ d. To talk to Lang

7. (A) After they ran out of the library, May Lee could *still feel the eyes looking at them*. What does that mean?

- ☐ a. She felt as if the people in the library were still staring at them.
- ☐ b. She thought that all the people in the library had run out after them.
- ☐ c. There was something the matter with May Lee's eyes.
- ☐ d. May Lee was asking Sue to look at something.

8. (C) What was the next thing that happened after Sue said she wanted to end it all?

- ☐ a. May Lee dragged her out of the library.
- ☐ b. May Lee and Sue got on a bus.
- ☐ c. Sue told May Lee she was going to see Lang.
- ☐ d. May Lee shook her.

9. (D) What did Sue find out from Lang's notebook?

- ☐ a. That Lang killed Clark
- ☐ b. Why she got headaches
- ☐ c. Why Lang didn't like her
- ☐ d. That she was not really hypnotized

10. (C) What was the last thing that happened?

☐ a. Sue found Lang's notebook.
☐ b. May Lee opened the door to Lang's office.
☐ c. Lang got out of the elevator.
☐ d. Sue and May Lee got out of the elevator.

Skills Used to Answer Questions
A. Recognizing Words in Context   B. Recalling Facts
C. Keeping Events in Order   D. Making Inferences
E. Understanding Main Ideas

Double Consonants: Part Two

In the last lesson, you learned that when you add a suffix that begins with a vowel to a one-syllable root that ends in a single vowel and a single consonant, then you must double the final consonant of the root. But what do you do if you have a root of more than one syllable? That is what you will learn in this chapter.

Stressed Syllables

A word often has two or more sounds, or *syllables.* You can hear the syllables when you say the word. Read the words below. Say each word out loud.

visit

control

abandon

You can hear two syllables when you say control (con-trol) and visit (vis-it). You can hear three syllables when you say abandon (a-ban-don).

You can also hear a change in your voice when you say the parts of each word. One syllable is stronger than all the others. The strongest syllable is called the *stressed syllable.* For example, say the word *visit.* The first sound, *vis,* is stronger. The stress in *visit* is on the first syllable. Now say *control.* The *trol* sound is stressed. Now say the word *abandon.* The second syllable, *ban,* is strongest. It is the stressed syllable.

Look at the roots, suffixes and new words below.

control + -ing = controlling

visit + -ing = visiting

abandon + -ing = abandoning

The words *control, visit,* and *abandon* all end in a single vowel and a single consonant. The suffix *-ing* begins with a vowel. Look at the word *control.* The final consonant, *l,* is doubled to make the word *controlling.* But look at the word *visit.* When adding the suffix *-ing* to make the word *visiting,* the final consonant is *not* doubled. Look at the word *abandon.* The final consonant is not doubled when adding *-ing* to make *abandoning.*

You know that in *control,* the stressed syllable is *trol.* It is the last syllable in the word. In *visit,* the stressed syllable is *vis,* which is the first syllable. In *abandon,* the stressed syllable is *ban,* the middle syllable.

In roots of more than one syllable, you double the final consonant *only* when the stress is on the last syllable.

Spelling Rule #4: When adding a suffix to a word of more than one syllable that ends in a consonant, double the final consonant if
   (a) the root ends in a single vowel and a single consonant, and
   (b) the stress is on the last syllable of the root, and
   (c) the suffix begins with a vowel.

Exercise 1

Look at the list of words below. Each word is broken into its separate sounds, or syllables. Say each word out loud. Which syllable is stressed in each word? Print the stressed syllable on the line to the right of the word. The first two have been done for you as examples.

1. flavor   fla vor   <u>*fla*</u>

2. regret   re gret   <u>*gret*</u>

3. butter   but ter   _____

4. prohibit   pro hib it   _____

5. propel   pro pel   _____

6. travel   trav el   _____

7. patrol   pa trol   _____

Exercise 2

On the next page is a list of roots and suffixes. All the roots have two or more syllables. They all end in a single vowel and a single consonant. All the suffixes begin with a vowel. Put the roots and suffixes together to make new words. Follow these steps:

1. Say each root word out loud to yourself. Decide which syllable is stressed. If it is the first syllable in the word, print *F* in the box next to the word. If

it is the middle syllable, print *M* in the box. If the
last syllable is the stressed syllable, print *L* in the
box.

2. Put the root and the suffix together. Double the
final consonant of the root if you have printed *L* in
the box next to it. Otherwise, make no spelling
change.

3. Print the new word on the line provided.

The first two have been done for you.

1. flavor $\boxed{F}$ flavor + -ing *Flavoring*

2. regret $\boxed{L}$ regret + -able *regrettable.*

3. excel $\boxed{}$ excel + -ent _____

4. forbid $\boxed{}$ forbid + -en _____

5. discover $\boxed{}$ discover + -y _____

6. begin $\boxed{}$ begin + -ing _____

7. batter $\boxed{}$ batter + -ed _____

Taxable Income

You have learned how to choose the tax form that is right for you. You also know how to enter your filing status and exemptions on a tax form. Now you will learn how to figure out your *taxable income*. That is the amount of your income on which you must pay income tax. In this lesson you will be shown how to enter your taxable income on form 1040EZ.

Gross Income and Taxable Income

Your *gross income* is the total amount of money you earned in a year. Your *taxable income* is the part of your gross income that you must pay taxes on. On a tax return, you begin by figuring your gross income and then work down to your taxable income.

Suppose you use form 1040EZ. You would use that form if you were single with no dependents and you had no special types of income or deductions. It is the easiest form to use. The taxable income sections of form 1040EZ are shown on the left.

To find your taxable income, you would follow these steps:

1. On line 1, write the amount of money you earned from your job for the year. You will find that amount in box 10 on your Wage and Tax Statement, or W-2 form. The taxpayer in the example earned $12,200 in wages.
2. On line 2, write the amount of interest you earned on your savings account. You will find that amount on the statement of payment sent to you by your

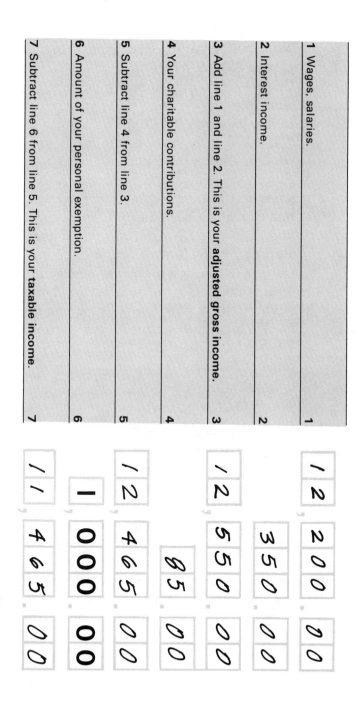

1 Wages, salaries.	**1**	12 200 00
2 Interest income.	**2**	1 350 00
3 Add line 1 and line 2. This is your **adjusted gross income.**	**3**	12 550 00
4 Your charitable contributions.	**4**	85 00
5 Subtract line 4 from line 3.	**5**	12 465 00
6 Amount of your personal exemption.	**6**	1 000 00
7 Subtract line 6 from line 5. This is your **taxable income.**	**7**	11 465 00

bank or credit union. The taxpayer in the example earned $350 in interest.

3. On line 3, enter the sum of your job earnings and your interest income. This is your *gross income*. In the example, the taxpayer's gross income is $12,550. That is the sum of $12,200 and $350.
4. On line 4, enter the amount of money you gave to churches, schools and other charities. The taxpayer in the example gave $85 to charity.
5. Subtract line 4 from line 3. Write your answer on line 5. In the example, $85 is subtracted from $12,550. So line 5 reads $12,465.
6. On line 6, the figure 1,000 is written in for you. That is the amount of your personal exemption.
7. Subtract line 6 from line 5. Enter your answer on line 7. The number on line 7 is your *taxable income*. The taxpayer in the example has a taxable income of $11,465.

Other Tax Forms

As you know, not all taxpayers can use form 1040EZ. People who are married or who have dependents must use form 1040 or 1040A. Those who have special types of income must use form 1040. Form 1040 and 1040A are longer than form 1040EZ. On those forms, you must also enter all special earnings and special deductions. But the basic steps are the same. You figure your gross income by adding all the money you have earned for the year. You then figure your taxable income by subtracting all your exemptions and deductions from your gross income.

Figuring Taxable Income

You know that your taxable income is the part of your income on which you must pay taxes. It is your gross income minus the exemptions and deductions you claim. You figure your gross income and your taxable income by filling out your tax return form. Here are the steps to follow to fill out form 1040EZ.

1. Find your total job earnings in box 10 of your W-2 form.
2. Find your interest earnings on the statement of payment sent to you by your bank or credit union.
3. Add your job earnings and your interest income to get your gross income.
4. Subtract any money you gave to charity.
5. Subtract $1,000 for your personal exemption.
6. You now have your taxable income. Enter that amount on your income tax return.

Exercise 1

The taxpayers in this exercise are all using form 1040EZ. Show how you would figure the gross income of each taxpayer. Remember that gross income is the person's total earnings plus interest on bank accounts. Write your answers in the spaces provided. The first one has been done for you as an example.

1. Richard Lake has two jobs. He earned $4,560 from one job. He earned $8,540 from his other job. He earned $350 in interest on his savings account.

   Richard Lake's gross income is _4,560_ + _8,540_ + _350_ .

2. Martha Randall earned $11,300 from her job. She earned $200 in interest on one savings account. She earned $100 in interest on a second bank account.

   Martha Randall's gross income is _____ + _____ + _____ .

3. Andrew Saks earned $6,890 from his job. He does not have a bank account.

   Andrew Saks's gross income is _____ .

4. Robert Tyler earned $15,350 from his job. He earned $300 in interest on his savings account.

   Robert Tyler's gross income is _____ + _____ .

5. Ann Harris earned $32,500 from her regular job. She also earned $500 for a one-time job she did for another company. She earned $275 in interest on her savings account.

   Ann Harris's gross income is _____ + _____ + _____ .

Exercise 2

Figure the taxable income of each of the taxpayers in this exercise. Taxable income on form 1040EZ is gross income minus gifts to charity and the taxpayer's personal exemption. Write your answers in the spaces provided. You may need to do the arithmetic on a separate piece of paper. The first one has been done for you as an example.

1. Richard Lake's gross income is $13,450. He gave $75 to charity. His personal exemption is $1,000. Richard Lake's taxable income is:

   <u>13,450</u>   -   <u>75</u>   - <u>1,000</u>   = <u>12,375</u> .

2. Martha Randall's gross income is $11,600. She gave $100 to charity. Her personal exemption is $1,000. Martha Randall's taxable income is:

   <u>   </u> - <u>   </u> - <u>   </u> = <u>   </u> .

3. Andrew Saks's gross income is $6,890. He gave nothing to charity. His personal exemption is $1,000. Andrew Saks's taxable income is:

   <u>   </u> - <u>   </u> = <u>   </u> .

Exercise 3

Below is information about a taxpayer's income and deductions. Use the information to fill out the taxable income section of form 1040EZ that follows. Follow the directions on the tax form to find the amounts that should be entered on lines 3, 5 and 7.

Wages: $10,500
Interest Income: $300
Charitable Contributions: $20
Personal Exemption: $1,000

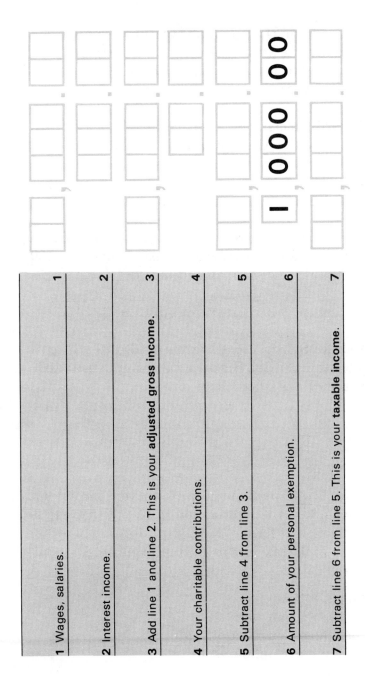

1 Wages, salaries.	1
2 Interest income.	2
3 Add line 1 and line 2. This is your adjusted gross income.	3
4 Your charitable contributions.	4
5 Subtract line 4 from line 3.	5
6 Amount of your personal exemption.	6
7 Subtract line 6 from line 5. This is your taxable income.	7

The Trance
Is Broken

Study the words in the box. Then read the sentences below with your teacher. Look carefully at the words in boldface type.

breakfast	fingerprints	meant	station
caught	growled	Ms.	trapped
children	hugged	policeman	truth
clues	lab	radio	twisted
confessed	lawyer	silent	whispered

1. They were **trapped** in his office!
2. What would he do to them if he **caught** them?
3. "Did you hear that?" she **whispered**.
4. Lang had **twisted** Sue's arm around in back of her.
5. "You'll never see your friend again," Lang **growled**.
6. "Two girls?" the **policeman** asked.
7. I'm afraid the **truth** is not very nice.
8. You have the right to be **silent**.
9. He turned on his **radio**.
10. Soon they were on their way to the police **station**.
11. Do you want to call a **lawyer**?
12. This is **Ms.** Howe.
13. I'll get the **lab** to have another look at Clark's body.
14. That may give us some **clues**.
15. Mr. Clark was always yelling at him when they were **children**.
16. A policeman came in with some **breakfast** for her.
17. We took Lang's **fingerprints**.
18. He **confessed** to killing his brother.
19. I never **meant** for things to happen this way.
20. As they walked out of the police station, May Lee **hugged** Sue.

Sue and May Lee looked at each other. Lang was coming! They were trapped in his office! What would he do to them if he caught them?

At the same moment, they both turned and ran through the dark into the other room. They quickly hid behind the big curtains that hung by the windows.

Lang came down the hall. When he saw that his office door was open, he stopped for a moment, then ran toward it. Carefully, he stuck his head into the office, then reached in, turned on the light and looked all around. At last he stepped into the office.

"Well," he said to himself, "someone was here, all right, but they're gone now. What did they want?" He walked over to his desk and looked at his papers. "My notebook! My notebook is gone! What's going on here? Why would anyone want to take my notebook?" While Lang walked up and down the office talking out loud to himself, May Lee and Sue held their breath behind the curtains. Sue's heart was beating so loudly that she was almost afraid that Lang would hear it.

"Maybe it was the police!" Lang said suddenly. "Maybe the police took the notebook. Is this some kind of trap? They let me go. They said they'd be coming to check out my office again, but if they've already been here they must know about me! They must know about Robert! What am I going to do? The police will be here soon! I have to get out of here before they get back!" Suddenly he ran toward the door.

Behind the curtains, May Lee poked Sue and whispered, "Did you hear that? Robert! That's Mr. Clark's first name! He called him Robert. That means that Lang knew Mr. Clark! That means—"

"What's that? Who's there?" Just as suddenly, Lang had come back into the office. He walked slowly into the other room and turned on the light. "Who's there?" he asked again. "Come out!"

May Lee and Sue stood still, holding their breath. Sue's heart was beating so loudly she thought it might burst.

Lang walked slowly across the room. He stopped for a moment, then threw back the curtains.

May Lee and Sue ran, but Lang was ready for them. He grabbed Sue and held her. May Lee stopped in the doorway and looked back, trying to think of what to do next. Lang twisted Sue's arm around in back of her, hard. "Ow! Stop it!" Sue yelled.

"What were you two girls doing in here?" Lang asked. "My notebook! *You* had it!" He grabbed the notebook away from Sue, shouting, "I'll get you for this!"

"Ow!" Sue yelled. "Quick, May Lee, run! Go get help!"

"If you go, you'll never see your friend again," Lang growled.

May Lee stayed in the doorway, ready to run, ready to fight, but afraid that whatever she did would be the wrong thing. Then a voice behind her said suddenly, "Police!"

"Oh, Officer, I'm so glad you're here," Lang told the policeman quickly. "I caught these two girls in my office! They broke in!"

"No, no, don't listen to him!" Sue yelled. "He's a murderer! He murdered Robert Clark!"

The policeman looked at her in surprise. "What's going on here?"

"I guess I'll have to tell you the truth," Lang said. "I have been trying to protect this girl, but I can see that it won't work. You see, Officer, this girl has been coming to my office every week so that I could hypnotize her to try to find out why she got headaches. I never did find out why. Then last night her boss, Robert Clark, broke into the office while she was here. She took a paperweight off my desk and hit him over the head, killing him. I know that I should have told this to the police right away, but I felt that since she had been hypnotized earlier—"

"No! No! He's lying! He *did* find out about my headaches!" Sue said. "It's all in his notebook!"

"What notebook?" Lang asked. "I don't have a notebook. You see? She—"

"I'm going to have to take you all in," the policeman cut in. "You're going to have to answer some more questions, Lang."

"Oh, of course," Lang said to the policeman, smiling

politely. "I just want to get all this cleared up."

The policeman looked at May Lee and Sue. "Remember," he told them, "you have the right to be silent. Anything you say may be used against you. Now come along, all three of you." He took them out of the office and down the hall.

The policeman took them to his car, where another policeman was waiting. The first policeman put May Lee and Sue in the back seat, then turned on his radio and called another police car to come and get Lang. Soon they were on their way to the police station. May Lee turned to Sue and said, "I can't believe this is happening!"

"I'm sorry I got you into this," Sue told her.

"Oh, that's OK. I was the one who got you into it in the first place. Do you think they'll lock us up? And Lorenzo Lang—are they going to do anything to him, or just ask him some questions?"

"We have to get them to believe us," Sue said. "We just have to!"

"Well, I'm glad to see that you have some fight in you again," May Lee said.

When they got to the police station, the policemen took them inside. They took Sue into a room by herself, while May Lee was taken into another room. They didn't see Lang anywhere.

"Do you want to call a lawyer?" the policeman asked Sue.

"I don't care. I just want to tell you what happened. Well, I don't really *know* what happened. You see, I was hypnotized. But I want to tell you everything that I can remember."

"You say you were hypnotized? Wait just a minute." The policeman called in a man to write down what Sue said. Then he called in a woman, too. "This is Ms. Howe," he told Sue. "She knows a lot about hypnotism. I thought that she should hear your story."

Sue told them the story, starting with the first time she saw Lang. She told them about her headaches. She told them everything that Lang had said to her. Then she told them about the night before, when Clark was killed. "When I woke up, I had a big glass paperweight in my hands," she told them. "Mr. Clark was lying on the floor. Mr. Lang told me that I killed him. Then he told me to go home. He said that he would tell the police that Mr. Clark had had a heart attack."

"You didn't see Clark come in?" Ms. Howe asked.

"No. He wasn't there when I went into the trance. And when I woke up, he was already dead."

"Do you know why Clark followed you to Lang's office?"

"No. I never told him that I was going there," Sue said. "I don't know why he came."

Ms. Howe turned to the policeman and said, "I think we're on to something here. We'd better follow up on this."

The policeman nodded. "I'll get some of our people on it right away," he said. "I'll get someone to talk to the people in Clark's office. Someone should go talk to Clark's wife again, too. And I'll talk to the lab about Clark's body again." He hurried out of the room.

Ms. Howe turned back to Sue and asked, "Would you like to find out what happened while you were in the trance?"

"Oh, yes!" Sue said. "But how? I can't remember anything."

"That is because Lang told you not to remember," Ms. Howe said. "But I am a hypnotist too. I can hypnotize you and tell you to remember everything that happened. Then you will remember it."

"Oh please, yes!" Sue said.

"What if you did do it?" Ms. Howe asked. "What if you remember that you did kill Clark?"

Sue thought for a moment. At last she said, "I just want to know."

"All right. Just sit back in your chair and relax. Let all the thoughts go out of your mind. Just think about my voice. Let yourself go. Let yourself relax. You are feeling very sleepy—"

When Sue was in a deep trance at last, Ms. Howe said, "You are now in Lang's office. Your boss has just come in. Can you see him?"

"No, he is standing over there." Without turning her head, Sue pointed to her right.

"Can you hear his voice?"

"Yes."

"What is he saying?" Ms. Howe asked.

"He is talking to Mr. Lang," Sue said. "He is asking what Mr. Lang has done to me." Sue stopped talking and sat silently.

"Now what is happening?" Ms. Howe asked.

"Mr. Lang is talking. He says that Mr. Clark was always yelling at him when they were children."

"When they were children?" Ms. Howe asked. "Are they brothers?"

"Yes."

"OK, now what is happening?"

"Mr. Clark says that Mr. Lang is hurting the Moving and Storage Company," Sue said. "He says that Mr. Lang hypnotized me and told me to give him the keys to the warehouse."

"Is that true?" Ms. Howe asked. "Did he tell you to give him the keys?"

"No, he told me to open the warehouse at night. He

also told me to put a new seal on the truck after it had been opened."

Ms. Howe turned to the policeman who was writing down what Sue was saying. "Are you getting all this down?" she asked.

"I sure am!" the policeman said.

Ms. Howe turned to Sue again and asked, "Now what is happening?"

"They are both yelling. Mr. Clark is saying, 'I'll get you for this!' Now they are running into the other room. They— Oh, no!" Sue put her hands over her face and started to cry.

"What is it? What happened?" Ms. Howe asked.

"I don't know," Sue cried. "I heard a sound . . . something hitting someone . . . and then someone fell down. Now Mr. Lang is telling me to get up." As she spoke, Sue stood up and walked forward. "He is putting the paperweight in my hands," she said, reaching out as if to take something. "Now he is telling me to wake up."

Ms. Howe walked up and down for a moment. "Wait until they hear this!" she said to the policeman. "*This* will show them that the police need hypnotists! This is great!" She turned to Sue and said, "When I say 'Wake up,' you will remember everything that you have told us today. OK, wake up."

Sue woke up. She jumped up and looked around her. Then she grabbed both of Ms. Howe's hands and shook them, crying, "Oh, thank you! Thank you! I know what happened now! And I didn't do it!"

"No, it doesn't look that way," Ms. Howe smiled. "Well, we have some work to do. You will have to wait here. Why don't you try to get some sleep?" Ms. Howe went out along with the policeman.

Sue walked up and down the room, thinking about everything that had happened. At last she fell asleep in a chair. When she woke up it was morning, and a policeman was coming in with some breakfast for her. She asked him for something to read, and he got her a newspaper.

At noon Ms. Howe came in, smiling from ear to ear. May Lee was with her, puffing excitedly on a cigarette. "Well, Sue, you're free to go," Ms. Howe said. "We checked with the Moving and Storage Company, and you were right—both of those trucks had been given a new seal. When we took Lang's fingerprints, we found out that he is really Will Clark, Robert's brother. Then we checked with the lab. The marks on Robert Clark's head showed that he *had* been hit with something. It could have been a paperweight. But the marks were very high. The person who hit him was much taller than you are."

May Lee burst in, "When they told it to Lang, he broke down and confessed!"

"Yes," Ms. Howe said. "Will Clark—or Lorenzo Lang—has confessed to killing his brother. So you are free to go."

"I can go," Sue said quietly. "I should go to work. Do you think I still have a job?" she asked May Lee.

"Of course you do!" May Lee said. "I was at work this morning—I'm on my lunch hour now—and I told them about what happened to you. I heard the supervisor talking about what a good worker you are. But, Sue, there's more! Lang wants to talk to you!"

"Mr. Lang wants to talk with *me?*" Sue asked.

"Yes," Ms. Howe said. "Will you see him?"

"All right," Sue said slowly, and Ms. Howe went out. A moment later, two policemen came in, with Lang between them. May Lee grabbed Sue's hand and held it. "What do you want?" Sue asked.

"I wanted to tell you that I am sorry about all this," Lang said.

"Well," Sue said in a cold voice, "it was an awful thing to do to someone."

"I know. I never meant for things to happen this way. I never thought my brother would follow you. But—that's all over now. I just wanted you to know that I *was* going to help you. When it was all over, I was going to tell you about your father. I did want to help you get rid of your headaches."

"I see," Sue said. "Thank you." She turned to May Lee and said. "Let's go. I want to get some lunch."

As they walked out of the police station, May Lee hugged Sue. "How could you talk to Lang?" she asked.

"You even *thanked* him! I would have wanted to hit him. How could you be so nice to him?"

"Now, now. He helped you, didn't he?" Sue asked. "You aren't afraid of dogs anymore. Maybe I should send you back to him and ask him to make you give up those cigarettes!"

"Never!" May Lee said.

"I'm only kidding," Sue said. "But he *was* a good hypnotist. He got me back with my father. He did help me get rid of my headaches." She smiled up at the sky and held her arms out wide. "But I'm sure glad it's all over," she said.

Directions. Answer these questions about the chapter you have just read. Put an *x* in the box beside the best answer to each question.

1. (C) What happened next after Lang found that his notebook was gone?

   ☐ a. A policeman came.
   ☐ b. Lang heard May Lee.
   ☐ c. Sue and May Lee ran.
   ☐ d. Lang started to run from his office. .

2. (D) Why didn't May Lee run away when Lang caught Sue?

   ☐ a. She knew that Lang wasn't after her.
   ☐ b. She was afraid that Lang would kill Sue.
   ☐ c. She didn't know where the door was.
   ☐ d. She couldn't move because she was in a deep trance.

3. (D) What did Ms. Howe think she would find out when she hypnotized Sue?

   ☐ a. That Sue was lying
   ☐ b. That Sue had killed Clark
   ☐ c. That Sue had not killed Clark
   ☐ d. That Clark was not dead

4. (A) After she heard Sue's story, Ms. Howe told the policeman, "We'd better *follow up on this*." What did she mean?

   □ a. We should get a detective to follow Lang.
   □ b. We should be the next ones in line.
   □ c. We should find out more about this.
   □ d. We should go upstairs after her.

5. (C) Which of these things happened last?

   □ a. Ms. Howe hypnotized Sue.
   □ b. The policeman took Sue to the police station.
   □ c. Lang confessed to killing Clark.
   □ d. The police told Lang all the clues they had found.

6. (E) What was the main thing that Sue found out in this part of the story?

   □ a. She didn't kill Robert Clark.
   □ b. Lang knew Robert Clark.
   □ c. Lang's real name was Will Clark.
   □ d. Ms. Howe was a hypnotist.

7. (B) How did the police find out who Lang really was?

   □ a. They asked Clark's wife.
   □ b. They looked in Lang's notebook.
   □ c. They looked in Lang's office.
   □ d. They checked Lang's fingerprints.

8. (B) How did the police know that Sue had not hit Clark?

☐ a. The marks on his head showed that he was hit by a taller person.
☐ b. The lab could not find any marks on his head.
☐ c. The marks on his body showed that he had been dead for two days.
☐ d. The lab told the police that Clark had not been hit.

9. (A) Sue spoke to Lang *in a cold voice.* How did she sound?

☐ a. As if she liked him
☐ b. As if she was afraid of him
☐ c. As if she was very mad at him
☐ d. As if she didn't want to be with him

10. (E) What was the main reason that Sue thanked Lang at the end of the story?

☐ a. He had helped her get rid of her headaches.
☐ b. She just wanted to be nice to him.
☐ c. He had kept her from going to jail.
☐ d. She wanted him to make May Lee stop smoking.

Skills Used to Answer Questions
A. Recognizing Words in Context   B. Recalling Facts
C. Keeping Events in Order   D. Making Inferences
E. Understanding Main Ideas

Words Ending in a Consonant and y

In this lesson you will learn how to spell words made by adding a suffix to a root ending in a consonant and the letter *y*.

Look at the roots, suffixes and new words below.

beauty + -ful = beautiful

empty + -ed = emptied

marry + -ing = marrying

All the root words end in a consonant followed by *y*. The suffix *-ful,* which is added to *beauty,* begins with a consonant. Look at the word *beautiful.* You can see that the *y* at the end of *beauty* was changed to *i* to make the new word.

The suffix *-ed,* which is added to *empty,* begins with a vowel. Look at the new word *emptied.* You can see that the *y* at the end of *empty* was changed to *i* when the suffix was added.

Now look at the last example. The suffix *-ing* begins with a vowel, but that vowel is *i*. Notice that in the word *marrying,* the final *y* in *marry* is not changed to *i*. When a suffix beginning with *i* is added to a root word ending in a consonant and *y*, there is no spelling change.

When adding a suffix to any root word ending in a consonant followed by *y*, you must first change the *y* to *i*, unless the suffix begins with *i*.

Now look at these roots, suffixes and new words.

play + -ful = playful

play + -ed = played

The root *play* ends in a vowel and the letter *y*. There is no spelling change in the new words *playful* and *played*. If a root ends in a vowel and *y*, make no spelling change.

Spelling Rule #5: When adding a suffix to a root word that ends in *y*, change the *y* to *i* if
  (a) the root ends in a consonant and *y*, and
  (b) the suffix begins with any letter other than *i*.

Exercise 1

Make new words from the roots and suffixes below. All the roots end in a consonant and *y*. None of the endings begin with *i*. Remember to change the *y* in the root to *i* before adding the suffix. Print the new word on the line provided. The first one has been done for you.

1. marry + -ed ___married___

2. happy + -ly _____

3. bury + -al _____

4. silly + -ness _____

5. worry + -ed _____

6. history + -cal _____

7. pity + -ful _____

8. try + -ed _____

Exercise 2

Make new words from the roots and suffixes below. All the roots end in a consonant and *y*. If the suffix begins with *i*, make no spelling change in the new word. Simply put the root and the suffix together. Otherwise, change the final *y* to *i* before adding the suffix. Print the new word on the line provided. The first two have been done for you.

1. copy + -ed   copied
2. copy + -ing   copying
3. study + -ing _____
4. pity + -ing _____
5. carry + -ed _____
6. carry + -ing _____
7. carry + -age _____
8. merry + -ment _____

Exercise 3

Combine the roots and endings below to make new words. Some of the roots end in a consonant and *y*. Some end in a vowel and *y*. To make new words, follow these steps.

1. Look at the spelling of the root. If it ends in a consonant and *y*, print *C* in the box next to it. If the root ends in a vowel and *y*, print *V* in the box.
2. Add the suffix to the root. If you have printed *C* in the box, change the *y* to *i* before adding the suffix. If you have printed *V* in the box, make no spelling change. Just add the suffix.
3. Print the new word on the line provided.

The first two have been done for you.

1. copy   [C]   copy + -ed   copied _____

2. stay   [V]   stay + -ed   stayed _____

3. hurry   [ ]   hurry + -ed _____

4. merry   [ ]   merry + -ly _____

5. employ   [ ]   employ + -er _____

6. happy   [ ]   happy + -ness _____

7. pray   [ ]   pray + -ed _____

8. enjoy   [ ]   enjoy + -ment _____

Tax Tables

You now know how to figure your taxable income. Once you know your taxable income, you are ready to figure out how much tax you must pay.

The federal government prints tax tables to make it easy for taxpayers to figure their taxes. Part of a tax table is shown below.

If line 7 (taxable income) is—		And you are—			
At least	But less than	Single	Married filing jointly	Married filing separately	Head of a household
				Your tax is—	
8,000					
8,000	8,050	764	543	875	697
8,050	8,100	771	550	884	704
8,100	8,150	779	557	893	711
8,150	8,200	786	564	902	718
8,200	8,250	794	571	911	725
8,250	8,300	801	578	920	732
8,300	8,350	809	585	929	739
8,350	8,400	816	592	938	746
8,400	8,450	824	599	947	753
8,450	8,500	831	606	956	760
8,500	8,550	839	613	965	767
8,550	8,600	847	620	974	774
8,600	8,650	855	627	983	781
8,650	8,700	863	634	992	788
8,700	8,750	871	641	1,001	795
8,750	8,800	879	648	1,010	804
8,800	8,850	887	655	1,019	812
8,850	8,900	895	662	1,028	821
8,900	8,950	903	669	1,037	829
8,950	9,000	911	676	1,046	838

Look first at the left column of the table. It is labeled *taxable income.* That column contains two long lists of numbers. One is labeled *At least.* The other is labeled *But less than.* In this column you look for the amount of your taxable income. It should lie between a number listed in the *At least* column and the one next to it in the *But less than* column. In other words, your taxable income should be at least as much as the first amount in the pair, but not more than the second amount.

Suppose your taxable income is $8,975. That is more than 8,950 but less than 9,000. It lies between the numbers 8,950 and 9,000 in the table. Find the line of the table that shows the numbers 8,950 and 9,000. That is your taxable income line.

Now look at the column on the right side of the table. It is labeled *And you are—.* The "and you are" refers to your filing status. Under the main label are the four possible filing statuses: single, married filing jointly, married filing separately, and head of household.

Find the correct column for your filing status. Suppose you are married and you and your spouse are filing separate returns. Find the column that is labeled *married filing separately.* Read down the column. Stop when you reach the number that is lined up with your taxable income line—8,950 and 9,000. Read the amount in the *married filing separately* column. The amount is 1,046. That is the amount you must pay in taxes.

Payment or Refund

You know that money is taken from each of your paychecks and sent to the government to pay for your taxes. You also know that your W-2 form tells you how much money the government has taken for taxes during the year. Sometimes the government has taken too much money. Then the government must *refund,* or pay back, the extra money. Sometimes the government has taken too little for taxes. Then you must send the government a check for the taxes you still owe.

So when you are figuring your income tax, you are looking for the answer to the question Do I owe the government money, or does the government owe me money?

To find out whether you paid too much or too little in taxes, follow these steps:
1. Look at the tax table and find your tax.
2. Look on your W-2 form at the box marked "Federal income tax withheld."
3. Compare your tax with the amount of money the government has withheld. If your tax is higher, then you owe the government money. If your tax is lower, then the government owes you money. You will get a refund.

Suppose your tax is $1,046. Your W-2 form says that the government took $1,600 from your earnings during the year. The amount that was withheld is higher than your tax. You paid in too much. The government will send you a check for $544 when you send in your tax return form.

Suppose your tax is $890. The government has taken $790 from your earnings. Your tax is higher than the amount that was withheld. Too little was taken from your earnings during the year. You must send the government a check for $100 for the tax you still owe.

Figuring Your Tax

Now you know how to use a tax table to find out how much income tax you must pay. You also know how to find out if you owe the government money or if the government owes you money.

Exercise 1

Part of a tax table is shown on the next page. Use the table to find out how much tax each person described in the exercise must pay. Follow these steps:

1. Find the person's taxable income on the left side of the table. Remember that the taxable income will be the same as or higher than the figure in the *At least* column. It will be lower than the figure in the *But less than* column.
2. Find the person's filing status on the right side of the table.
3. Read down the filing status column to the number that lines up with the person's taxable income line. That amount is the person's tax.
4. Write the amount of the person's tax on the line provided.

If line 7 (taxable income) is—		And you are—			
At least	But less than	Single	Married filing jointly	Married filing separately	Head of a household
			Your tax is—		

20,000

At least	But less than	Single	Married filing jointly	Married filing separately	Head of a household
20,000	20,050	3,212	2,466	3,937	2,972
20,050	20,100	3,225	2,475	3,954	2,984
20,100	20,150	3,238	2,484	3,970	2,996
20,150	20,200	3,251	2,493	3,987	3,008
20,200	20,250	3,264	2,503	4,003	3,020
20,250	20,300	3,277	2,514	4,020	3,032
20,300	20,350	3,290	2,525	4,036	3,044
20,350	20,400	3,303	2,536	4,053	3,056
20,400	20,450	3,316	2,547	4,069	3,068
20,450	20,500	3,329	2,558	4,086	3,080
20,500	20,550	3,342	2,569	4,102	3,092
20,550	20,600	3,355	2,580	4,119	3,104
20,600	20,650	3,368	2,591	4,135	3,116
20,650	20,700	3,381	2,602	4,152	3,128
20,700	20,750	3,394	2,613	4,168	3,140
20,750	20,800	3,407	2,624	4,185	3,152
20,800	20,850	3,420	2,635	4,201	3,164
20,850	20,900	3,433	2,646	4,218	3,176
20,900	20,950	3,446	2,657	4,234	3,188
20,950	21,000	3,459	2,668	4,251	3,200

21,000

At least	But less than	Single	Married filing jointly	Married filing separately	Head of a household
21,000	21,050	3,472	2,679	4,267	3,212
21,050	21,100	3,485	2,690	4,284	3,224
21,100	21,150	3,498	2,701	4,300	3,236
21,150	21,200	3,511	2,712	4,317	3,248
21,200	21,250	3,524	2,723	4,333	3,260
21,250	21,300	3,537	2,734	4,350	3,272
21,300	21,350	3,550	2,745	4,366	3,284
21,350	21,400	3,563	2,756	4,383	3,296
21,400	21,450	3,576	2,767	4,399	3,308
21,450	21,500	3,589	2,778	4,416	3,320
21,500	21,550	3,602	2,789	4,432	3,332
21,550	21,600	3,615	2,800	4,449	3,344
21,600	21,650	3,628	2,811	4,465	3,356
21,650	21,700	3,641	2,822	4,482	3,368
21,700	21,750	3,654	2,833	4,498	3,380
21,750	21,800	3,667	2,844	4,515	3,392
21,800	21,850	3,680	2,855	4,531	3,404
21,850	21,900	3,693	2,866	4,548	3,416
21,900	21,950	3,706	2,877	4,564	3,428
21,950	22,000	3,719	2,888	4,581	3,440

The first one has been done for you as an example.

1. Carl and Sharon Jackson
    Filing Status: Married filing jointly
    Taxable Income: 21,935

    Their tax is ___2,877_____

2. Laura Parker
    Filing Status: Single
    Taxable Income: 20,350

    Her tax is _____

3. Wendy Gardner
    Filing Status: Head of household
    Taxable Income: 20,940

    Her tax is _____

4. John Scott
    Filing Status: Married filing separately
    Taxable Income: 21,320

    His tax is _____

5. Stuart and Linda Crane
    Filing Status: Married filing jointly
    Taxable Income: 21,975

    Their tax is _____

Exercise 2

Which of the people below still owe money to the government? Which of them will get a refund? To find out, follow these steps:

1. Look at each person's tax.
2. Look at the amount the government withheld from their earnings.
3. Compare the two amounts.
4. If the amount withheld is higher, the government must send the person a refund check. Print *Refund* on the line provided.
5. If the tax is higher, the person must send a check to the government for the rest of his or her taxes. Print *Payment* on the line.

The first two have been done for you as examples.

1. Mary Marks
   Tax: 1,200
   Amount Withheld: 1,000

   _Payment_____

2. Thomas Wilson
   Tax: 2,400
   Amount Withheld: 2,500

   _Refund_____

3. Henry Sikes
   Tax: 1,900
   Amount Withheld: 1,800

   _____

4. Gail Adams
   Tax: 2,450
   Amount Withheld: 3,000

   _____

5. Peter Booth
   Tax: 3,240
   Amount Withheld: 3,300

   _____

To the Instructor

Purpose of the Series

Teachers charged with the responsibility of providing instruction for adults and older students with reading difficulties face a major problem: the lack of suitable materials. Stories written at the appropriate level of maturity are too difficult; stories easy enough to read independently are too childish.

The stories in the Adult Learner Series were written to solve the readability problem. The plots and characters in these stories are suitable for adults and older students, yet the stories can be read easily by very low-level readers.

The principal goal of the series is to provide interest and enjoyment for these readers. To this end, every attempt has been made to create a pleasant reading experience and to avoid frustration. The plots move quickly but are kept simple; a few characters are introduced and developed slowly; the same characters are utilized throughout a text; sentence structure and vocabulary are carefully monitored.

A secondary goal is to help adults explore and develop everyday life skills. Lessons and exercises about a variety of life skills provide adults and older students with the basic competencies they need for success in this fast-paced world.

Rounding out the structure of the series are exercises for developing vocabulary skills, comprehension skills, and language skills.

Reading Level

The stories in the Adult Learner Series are all written at the second and third grade reading levels. The first six titles in the series range from mid-first to second grade level; the next three titles are at the high-second and third grade levels. It should be kept in mind, however, that the stories were written for adults: people with a wider range of experience and larger speaking and listening vocabularies than those of elementary school children. Thus, there are some words and some events which might present difficulties for elementary school students but which should not pose problems for older beginning readers.

Besides the slightly increased complexity of vocabulary and plot, the writing style itself has been adapted for older beginning readers. Every effort was made to make the prose sound natural while maintaining simplicity of structure and vocabulary. The repetition of words and phrases has been carefully controlled to permit maximum learning of new words without producing a childish effect.

The reading levels of the stories were established by applying Dr. Edward B. Fry's *Formula for Estimating Readability* and *3,000 Instant Words* by Elizabeth Sakiey and Edward Fry. *3,000 Instant Words* lists the 3,000 most common words in the English language, ranked in order of frequency. The first 100 words on the list and their common variants [*-s, -ing,* etc.] make up 50 percent of all written material. The first 300 words and their variants make up 65 percent of all written material. Because readers encounter a relatively small number of words so frequently, they must be able to recognize the Instant Words immediately to be effective readers.

The story line of *Killer in a Trance?* presents some concepts—office structure, the workings of a moving and storage company, hypnotism—that may be new to some students. A discussion of these concepts might improve comprehension and enhance the element of reading for pleasure which is the primary purpose of all the stories in the Adult Learner Series.

Structure and Use of the Text

Each book in the Adult Learner Series is divided into several units. Each unit follows a regular format consisting of these sections:

Preview Words

Twenty words from each chapter are presented for students to preview before reading. Those words that were expected to give students the most difficulty were chosen for previewing. The preview section includes all words of more than one syllable that are not among the first 2,000 words on Sakiey and Fry's list of 3,000 Instant Words. The words are listed first in alphabetical order and then shown again in story sequence in sentences based on the chapter.

The twenty sentences match the chapter in readability; students can read the sentences independently. With some classes the instructor may want to read the words and sentences aloud for students to repeat and learn. In very structured classes, the words could also be used for spelling and writing practice.

Story

The primary purpose of the story is to provide interesting material for adult readers. It should be read as a story; the element of pleasure should be present. Because of the third grade reading level, students should be able to read the story on their own.

Comprehension Questions

Ten multiple-choice comprehension questions follow

each chapter. There are two questions for each of these five comprehension skills:

A. Recognizing Words in Context
B. Recalling Facts
C. Keeping Events in Order
D. Making Inferences
E. Understanding Main Ideas

The letters *A* through *E* appear in the text as labels to identify the questions.

The comprehension questions are constructed to cover all parts of the chapter evenly and to bring out important points in the story. This insures that the student understands the story so far before going on to the next chapter.

Students should answer the questions immediately after reading the chapter and correct their answers using the key at the back of the book. Students should circle incorrect responses and check off correct ones.

The graphs at the back of the book help the instructor keep track of each student's comprehension progress. The *Comprehension Progress Graph* shows comprehension percentage scores. The *Skills Profile Graph* identifies areas of comprehension weakness needing special attention and extra practice.

Language Skills

These sections cover many aspects of language study: phonics, word attack skills, simple grammar, spelling rules, punctuation, and correct usage. The readability of these sections is higher than that of the chapters. The readability level varies depending on the vocabulary load of the specific language skill being taught.

Because the language skills are taught in clear and simple terms, most students will be able to work these sections independently. However, the instructor should be alert for opportunities to explain and further illustrate the content of the lessons.

The lessons contain exercises which give students the opportunity to practice the language skills being taught. An answer key at the back of the book makes it possible for students to correct their work.

Understanding Life Skills

Every chapter is accompanied by two sections which deal with life skills. The first, "Understanding Life Skills," introduces and fully explains a specific life skill. The life skills all revolve around some detail of modern adult life.

Because this section stresses *understanding* a certain life skill, the reading level is higher than the reading level of the story. However, the life skill lessons are presented in carefully prepared steps, and most students should be able to read and comprehend them without too much difficulty.

Questions used in the lessons are designed to focus the students' attention and to reinforce the learning. Answers for all questions are provided at the back of the book.

Applying Life Skills

Because modern-day living requires both *knowing* and *doing,* two life skills sections follow each chapter to emphasize both aspects. The second, "Applying Life Skills," is primarily a practical exercise.

This section builds on the understanding generated in the previous section. Students should be able to complete the exercise successfully by applying what they have just read.

Completing this section allows students to demonstrate their mastery of a specific life skill. It gives them the firsthand experience they need with tasks they are likely to encounter in everyday living.

An Answer Key at the back of the book helps students correct their work and gives them immediate feedback.

All units in each book are structured alike, each consisting of the six sections described here. Students quickly discover the regular pattern and are able to work with success and confidence throughout the text.

Use in Small-Group or Class Situations

Although the books in the Adult Learner Series were designed primarily for use on an individual basis, they can be used successfully in small-group or class situations. The comprehension, language and life skills questions can be adapted to whole-class instruction; this may be especially useful for students of English as a Second Language. If several students have read the stories, a group discussion may prove rewarding as well as motivating.

Writing Assignments

The comprehension questions and answers may also serve as suggestions for writing assignments.

For many students at this level, a writing assignment must be introduced in a very structured manner; otherwise, some students may find themselves unable to get started. On a group basis, the writing assignment may grow naturally out of the class discussion. In this case, the discussion may be all the introduction necessary.

On an individual basis, however, and also often within a group situation, it will be necessary to provide the student with a more concrete starting point. The teacher may find it necessary to provide model sentences or paragraphs, or to supply sentence beginnings ("If I had been there, I would have . . .") for the student to complete. The students can use their copies of the stories to search for word spellings, or the teacher may wish to write suggested words on the blackboard or provide a prepared list.

The Word List

Every word used in the story is included in the Word List, given alphabetically under the chapter in which it is first introduced. New forms that are made by adding the suffixes -s, -ed, -ing, and -ly to words that have already been introduced are indented.

The instructor may wish to scan the Word List to choose preview words in addition to the twenty in the Preview Words section at the beginning of each chapter. Non-phonetic words, which may present some difficulties in decoding, are printed in italics for quick identification.

The Word List may also be used for the study of common sight words. Since an effort has been made to provide adequate repetition of each word, most of these words should be a solid part of the student's sight vocabulary by the time he or she has finished reading the story.

Summary of the Chapters in Killer in a Trance?

Chapter 1: The Hypnotist (Level 3.0)

It is just minutes before closing on Friday afternoon at Clark's Moving and Storage Company, but Clark angrily demands that his employees stay till the last moment. Sue, who types up the supervisor's work orders, has a terrible headache. She gets headaches often. When they finally leave work, Sue's friend May Lee talks her into attending a hypnotism show. She wants her friend to relax and have fun. During the show, May Lee volunteers to be hypnotized, and Lorenzo Lang, the hypnotist, cures her of her fear of dogs by having her relive a child-hood trauma.

Chapter 2: Into a Trance (Level 3.0)

May Lee talks Sue into going to Lang for a cure for her headaches. Lang hypnotizes Sue, then orders her to go back to the warehouse at night and leave the door unlocked for one hour. He also tells her to return to him in one week.

Chapter 3: The Plan (Level 3.2)

Under post-hypnotic suggestions, Sue returns to the warehouse the next night. Two men hired by Lang enter the warehouse and steal silver from a loaded van. When the theft is discovered, Clark is livid. The following week, Sue returns for another appointment with Lang. Using hypnosis, Lang traces her headaches to a fear of losing her family's love, stemming from her mother's desertion when Sue was a child. Lang does not inform Sue of his discovery, but gives her the same set of instructions he gave her the week before. Once again, Sue lets the hired thieves into the warehouse.

Chapter 4: The Killer Strikes (Level 2.5)

The second theft is discovered the following morning. After raging at the supervisor, Clark hires detectives to follow Sue and two other employees who have keys to the warehouse. When Sue goes to Lang's office for her next appointment, Clark is notified. He follows her and confronts Lang. They quarrel, revealing that they are brothers. Lang kills Clark, then tells Sue that she committed the murder while in a trance.

Chapter 5: To End It All (Level 3.1)

The next day, depressed by her guilt, Sue sits at home. May Lee goes to visit her, and Sue tells her what happened. May Lee tries to convince her that she couldn't have done it. They go to the library to learn more about hypnosis, to see if Sue could have killed someone while in a trance. They learn that hypnotized people can be made to hurt others. Sue threatens suicide. Then she pulls herself together and she and May Lee decide to break into Lang's office to look for clues to what really happened. They find Lang's notebook, which tells them that Lang has discovered the cause of Sue's headaches. At that point, Lang enters his office.

Chapter 6: The Trance Is Broken (Level 3.0)

Lang finds Sue and May Lee with his notebook. He threatens Sue. Just in time, the police arrive on the scene. They take Sue, May Lee and the hypnotist to the police station for questioning. Sue tells her story to the police, who call in a police hypnotist. Under hypnosis, Sue recalls the true circumstances of the murder. Lang confesses, and Sue is free.

Words Introduced in the Story

Non-phonetic words are in italics. New forms of words already introduced are indented.

Chapter 1: The Hypnotist

a
about
afraid
after
again
against
age
ago
ahead
air
all
almost
alone
along
already
always
am
and
angrily
another
any
anyone
anything
are
aren't
arm
  arms
around
as
ask
  asked

asleep
at
ate
awake
away

back
bad
bare
bark
  barked
be
been
before
began
behind
bend
  bending
better
between
big
bit
black
blinked
blue
bowed
boy
breath
brother
  brother's
brown

Brownie
bugging
bumped
burst
but
butts
by

call
  called
  calling
came
can
can't
care
careful
  carefully
cat
  cats
chair
  chairs
change
chased
cheered
cigarette
city
clapped
  clapping
Clark
  Clark's
clock

closed
  closing
coat
  coats
coin
come
  comes
  coming
could
couldn't
count
course
cover
crazy
crowd
cry
  cried
  crying
cute

danger
dare
day
deep
desk
did
didn't
do
  doing
dock
doctor
  doctors
does
doesn't
dog
  dogs
  doggie
don't

door
down
drag
driving
dropped

ear
early
eat
eaten
even
every
everyone
everything
eyes

face
fall
far
father
feel
feet
fell
felt
few
first
five
flat
floor
foot
for
forehead
forget
forward
Friday
friend
  friendly
from

front
fun
fur

gasp
  gasped
  gasping
gave
get
  getting
girl
go
  going
gone
good
good-by
got
grabbed
great
groaned
grow
  growing
  grown

had
hadn't
hair
hand
  hands
happen
  happened
  happening
happy
hard
  harder
hate
have
he

he's
head
  heads
headache
  headaches
hear
heard
heavy
held
her
here
herself
high
him
himself
his
hold
  holding
home
hot
how
hurried
hurt
  hurting
hypnotist
hypnotize
  hypnotized

I
  I'm
  I've
  I'll
  I'd
if
in
into
is
isn't

it
  its
  it's

job
jump
  jumped
  jumping
just

keep
kept
killer
know
  knows
  known

laid
Lang
lap
last
laugh
  laughed
leave
led
Lee
  Lee's
left
let
  let's
lift
  lifted
light
like
listen
lit
little
loading

long
look
  looked
  looking
Lorenzo
lots
loudest
  loudly
low

made
main
make
man
  man's
may (May)
maybe
me
men
middle
minute
miss
  missed
moment
Monday
more
move
  moved
  moving
Mr.
much
must
my

near
never
new
next

nice
no
nod
  nodded
not
nothing
now

o'clock
of
off
office
oh
OK
old
on
once
one
onto
open
or
orders
other
  others
out
outside
over
overtime

papers
pat
  patted
  patting
pay
people
person
pile
  piled

place
  places
play
pointed
  pointing
pulled
  pulling
puppy
  puppies
purring
pushed
put
  putting

question
  questions
quickly
quiet
  quietly
quite

railing
ran
reached
ready
real
red
relax
  relaxed
remember
right
rims
row
rubbed
running

said
same

sat
saw
say
  saying
scare
  scared
seat
  seats
second
see
seem
seen
sent
she
shook
should
shouted
show
  showed
  shown
shut
sides
sidewalk
sit
  sitting
six
sleep
  sleepy
slowly
smaller
smiled
smoking
sniffing
so
soft
  softly
some
  something

soon
sound
  sounded
speak
stage
stairs
stand
  standing
stare
  staring
steep
step
  stepped
stepmother
stiff
  stiffly
still
stood
stop
  stopped
storage
straight
strange
street
stuck
suddenly
Sue
  Sue's
sure

tail
take
talk
  talked
  talking
tall
tell
  telling

ten
that
the
theater
their
them
then
there
  there's
these
they
thin
thing
  things
think
third
this
those
thought
  thoughts
three
threw
through
tight
time
tipped
tired
to
told
tonight
too
took
top
toward
trance
trucks
tried
turned

two
typed
  typing
typewriter

until
up
used

vans
very
voice

wagging
waited
  waiting
wake
  wakes
walk
  walked
  walking
wall
want
  wanted
  wants
warehouse
was
wasn't
wasting
watch
  watched
water
waving
way
we
  we're
week
weekend

well
went
were
what
when
where
while
who
why
wide
will
wished
with

woke
woman
women
won't
word
work
working
world
worried
worries
worse
would
wouldn't

year
years
yelling
yes
yet
you
you'd
you're
you've
your

Chapter 2: Into a Trance

able
address
an
answer
apartment
appointment
ashtray

because
below
blocks
body
boomed
boss
both
bowing
break
bright
bring
bringing

brushed
building
bus

calls
calm
card
carrying
case
catching
cause
causing
chain
charge
check
checkbook
chin
close
closely
company

covered
curtain
curtains
cut

dark
deeply
dig
dizzy
done
doors
doorbell
doorway
downstairs
dragged

each
elevator
else
end

example
excitedly

falling
fear
find
fine
fire
forgot
found

gets
give
gives
gold
grew
grouch

hallway
has
he'll
hello
help
here's
hope
hopefully
hour
hurrying
hypnotist's

idea
ideas
inside
itself

kind
knew

ladies
lamps
Lang's
late
lean
lie
lying
life
lighted
listened
listening
loaded
lot

Ma
mad
makes
many
match
maybe
mean
mind
minutes
morning
mother
mumbled

name
need
needed
nicer
night
notebook
notes

older
ones
only

opened
order
ow
our

pain
palms
paper
past
phone
pick
plan
pocketbook
poor
puffing
pulling
pushing

really
rest
rid
Robert
rode
room
rushed

sad
sadly
saying
says
scratched
scratching
seal
seemed
shall
she's
shy
sign

slammed
  sleepily
slept
  small
sorry
  sounds
spoke
start
  started
stay
  stayed
such
supervisor
surprised

table
than
thank
  that's
though

times
today
tomorrow
touch
trick
  truck
trust
try
turn
turning
type

under
understand
unlocked
us

visit

wait

walking
wastebasket
whatever
  what's
which
whole
window
  windows
wish
wondered
  worked
worth
wow
write
wrote

yawned
  yells
  yours

Chapter 3: The Plan

across
added
afternoon
  asking
awful

bag
  being
bed
begin
  beginning
begun
believe

belt
bet
bill
blames
blankets
  blink
bother
  bothers
boxes
  breaks
broke
button

cares
carrying
  changed
click
cool
  covers
creeps
crossed

Dad
  days

easier

evening

facing
family
fast
fears
feeling
fifty
fill
filled
flashlight
flashlights
foreman
full
funny

girl's
glad
goes
grabbing
greatest
gun

half
handed
happens
hasn't
haven't
headed
heading
helped
how's
hung
hungry

jobs

keys

kinds
kitchen

lately
later
leaned
lets
lock
locked
lose
lost
love
loves
lucky
lunch

Mama
matter
melt
met
missing
mouth

nail
nervous
normal
number

opening
own

paid
Papa
parked
part
passed
peeked
picked

pocket
pointing
pounding
pretty

quitting

raised
rats
reach
reason
report
rested
ringing
robbed
robbers
run

sealed
seals
seeing
sees
set
she'll
shined
shouldn't
shouting
side
silver
since
somehow
someone
sometime
somewhere
spend
squeeze
starting
stuff

supper   *touched*   van
         trigger
thinking   trying   watching
thinks   TV   without
throwing   *workers*
toes   unloaded   *worry*

Chapter 4: The Killer Strikes

anywhere   detectives   house
asking   doctor's   hurry
attack   dragging
   driver   kill
baby   *knock*
badly   *enough*
beat   lay
bent   finish   lead
best   flipped   letting
blame   follow   line
blow   followed   list
boring   following   *live*
breaking   fool   *lives*
breathe   fuse   locks
breathing   looks
   glass
calling   glumly   mess
checked   grab   *might*
chest
closer   hall   newspapers
corner   hated
crashed   *having*   Omar
   heap
dazed   *heart*   pale
dead   helping   *paperweight*
dear   hit   phoned
detective

police	sir	Tuesdays
purple	slow	
	smiling	*uncovered*
quick	spent	unless
	spotted	upstairs
race	stared	
rang	staying	visited
reported	stolen	
reports	strikes	we'd
roaring	sudden	we've
rob	Sunday	*weren't*
robberies	surprise	*wildly*
robbery		wonder
	taxi	worker
Saturday	telling	
screamed	*they'll*	yelled
send	thrown	*yourself*
shirt	thud	
short	Tuesday	

Chapter 5: To End It All

anyway	eating	hypnotism
	empty	
backward	encyclopedia	jail
block	ended	
book	excited	killed
books		
	fight	latest
croaked	finished	legs
	food	library
death	frame	*loses*
died		loud
downtown	hardly	luck
	he'd	
earlier	*hey*	means

money
most
murder
  murderer
myself

news
newspaper

page
  pages
please

questioning

read
  reading
ring

save
shaking
sick
sight
slipped
slumped
snap
  snapped
steps

stringing
sudden
surprising

taking
they're
true

waked
waking

yesterday
you'll

Chapter 6: The Trance Is Broken

beating
breakfast
  broken
brothers

car
caught
children
  cigarettes
clear
  cleared
cold
confessed

excitedly

fingerprints
free

girls
given
growled
guess

hid
  hidden
hitting
Howe
  Howe's
hugged
  hypnotists
hypnotizing

kidding
  killing

lab
lawyer

locking

marks
meant
Ms.
  murdered

noon

officer

poked
policeman
politely
protect

radio
  Robert's

silent
  silently

sky   *they've*   whisper
  station   trap   whispered
story   trapped   whispering
               truth   *who's*
  taken   twisted   wife
  taller   *writing*
  thanked   we'll   *wrong*

Answer Key

Comprehension Questions

Chapter 1
1. a	2. b	3. d	4. b	5. c
6. d	7. c	8. b	9. c	10. a

Chapter 2
1. a	2. c	3. a	4. b	5. b
6. d	7. c	8. a	9. b	10. d

Chapter 3
1. d	2. a	3. d	4. a	5. c
6. b	7. b	8. a	9. c	10. b

Chapter 4
1. a	2. c	3. b	4. a	5. b
6. d	7. c	8. a	9. d	10. b

Chapter 5
1. a	2. a	3. b	4. c	5. d
6. b	7. a	8. d	9. b	10. c

Chapter 6
1. d	2. b	3. c	4. c	5. c
6. a	7. d	8. a	9. d	10. a

Language Skills

Chapter 1: Exercise 1

1. trying
2. fairness
3. pavement
4. opening

5. parked
6. cupful
7. fitness
8. actor

Exercise 2

1. No Spelling Change
2. Spelling Change
3. Spelling Change
4. Spelling Change
5. No Spelling Change

6. No Spelling Change
7. Spelling Change
8. No Spelling Change
9. Spelling Change
10. No Spelling Change

Chapter 2: Exercise 1

1. skating
2. survival
3. giving
4. dictator

5. changed
6. coming
7. given
8. smoker

Exercise 2

1. V purify
2. C hopeless
3. V hoping
4. C careless
5. V caring
6. C careful

7. V engaging
8. C engagement
9. C useful
10. V using
11. V loving
12. C loveless

Chapter 3: Exercise 1

1. manageable
2. traceable
3. noticeable
4. changeable
5. serviceable

Exercise 2

1. valuable
2. danceable
3. quotable
4. pronounceable
5. livable
6. notable
7. chargeable
8. storable
9. exchangeable
10. movable

Exercise 3

1. placing
2. placeable
3. adoring
4. adorable
5. erased
6. erasable
7. serviceable
8. servicing
9. peaceful
10. peaceable
11. used
12. usable

Chapter 4: Exercise 1

1. redden
2. cutter
3. patted
4. stopping
5. hoggish
6. spotty

Exercise 2

1. dimly
2. dimmed
3. cupful
4. bitten
5. sappy
6. planner
7. fatten
8. fatness
9. reddish
10. hatless

Exercise 3

1. VVC reader
2. VC   rotten
3. CC   ending
4. VC   sunny
5. VVC hooting
6. VC cupped
7. VC thinner
8. CC winding
9. VC hidden
10. VC runner

Chapter 5: Exercise 1

1. fla
2. gret
3. but
4. hib
5. pel
6. trav
7. trol

Exercise 2

1. F flavoring
2. L regrettable
3. L excellent
4. L forbidden
5. M discovery
6. L beginning
7. F battered

Chapter 6: Exercise 1

1. married
2. happily
3. burial
4. silliness
5. worried
6. historical
7. pitiful
8. tried

Exercise 2

1. copied
2. copying
3. studying
4. pitying
5. carried
6. carrying
7. carriage
8. merriment

Exercise 3

1. C copied
2. V stayed
3. C hurried
4. C merrily
5. V employer
6. C happiness
7. V prayed
8. V enjoyment

Applying Life Skills

Chapter 1: Exercise 1

1. Gross Earnings
2. Witholding Tax Federal
3. Pay Period
4. Date
5. FICA
6. Net Pay

Exercise 2

1. 465.00
2. 581.15
3. 72.08
4. 33.04
5. 11.03
6. 465.00

Chapter 2: Exercise 1

1. $12,400.00
2. $1,990.00
3. $420.00
4. 183-45-9632
5. $1,230.00

Exercise 2

1. First National Savings Bank
2. Rose Perez
3. 51.50

Chapter 3: Exercise

1. 1040
2. 1040A
3. 1040A
4. 1040

5. 1040
6. 1040EZ
7. 1040A

Chapter 4: Exercise 1

1. 2.
2. 4
3. 2

4. 4
5. 2

Exercise 2

Step 2 **Check your** **filing status** (Check only one)	1 □ Single. 2 ☒ Married filing joint return. 3 □ Married filing separate return. 4 □ Head of household.		

Step 3
Figure your
exemptions

Always check the exemption box labeled Yourself. Check other boxes if they apply.

5a ☒ Yourself   □ 65 or over   □ Blind
b ☒ Spouse   □ 65 or over   □ Blind   Write number of boxes checked on 5a and b   **2**
c First names of your dependent children who lived with you _____

Attach Copy B of
Form(s) W-2 here

Jane Donald   Write number of children listed on 5c   **+2**

d Other dependents:

1. Name	2. Relationship

Write number of other dependents listed on 5d   +_____

e Total number of exemptions claimed.   Add numbers entered on lines above   **=4**

Chapter 5: Exercise 1

1. 4,560 + 8,540 + 350
2. 11,300 + 200 + 100
3. 6,890
4. 15,350 + 300
5. 32,500 + 500 + 275

Exercise 2

1. 13,450 – 75 – 1,000 = 12,375
2. 11,600 – 100 – 1,000 = 10,500
3. 6,890 – 1,000 = 5,890

Exercise 3

1 Wages, salaries.	1	$10,500.00
2 Interest income.	2	$300.00
3 Add line 1 and line 2. This is your **adjusted gross income**.	3	$10,800.00
4 Your charitable contributions.	4	$20.00
5 Subtract line 4 from line 3.	5	$10,780.00
6 Amount of your personal exemption.	6	$1,000.00
7 Subtract line 6 from line 5. This is your **taxable income**.	7	$9,780.00

Chapter 6: Exercise 1

1. 2,877
2. 3,303
3. 3,188

4. 4,366
5. 2,888

Exercise 2

1. Payment
2. Refund
3. Payment
4. Refund
5. Refund

Comprehension Progress Graph

How to Use the Comprehension Progress Graph

1. At the top of the graph, find the number of the chapter you have just read.
2. Follow the line down until it crosses the line for the number of questions you got right.
3. Put a dot • where the lines cross.
4. The numbers on the other side of the graph show your comprehension score.

For example, this graph shows the score of a student who answered 7 questions right for Chapter 1. The score is 70%.

This same student got scores of 80% and 90% on Chapters 2 and 3. The line connecting the dots keeps going up. This shows that the student is doing well.

If the line between the dots on your graph does not go up, or if it goes down, see your instructor for help.

Comprehension Progress

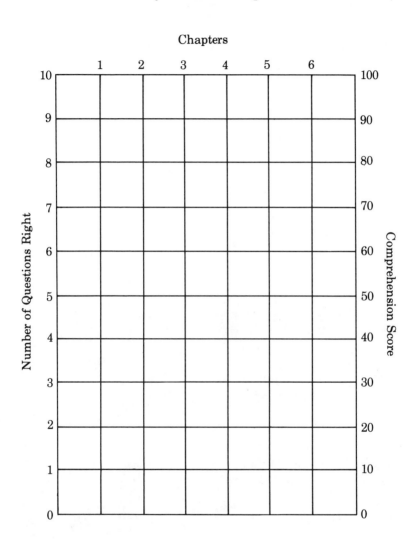

Skills Profile Graph

How to Use the Skills Profile Graph

1. There is a block on this graph for every comprehension question in the book.
2. Every time you get a question wrong, fill in a block which has the same letter as the question you got wrong. For example, if you get an A question wrong, fill in a block in the A row. Use the right row for each letter.

Look at the graph. It shows the profile of a student who got 3 questions wrong. This student got an A question wrong, a C question wrong, and a D question wrong.

On the next chapter, this same student got 4 questions wrong and has filled in 4 more blocks.

The graph now looks like this. This student seems to be having trouble on question C. This shows a reading skill that needs to be worked on.

The blocks that are filled in on your graph tell you and your instructor the kinds of questions that give you trouble.

Look for the rows that have the most blocks filled in.

These rows will be higher than the others. Talk to your instructor about them. Your instructor may want to give you extra help on these skills.

Skills Profile

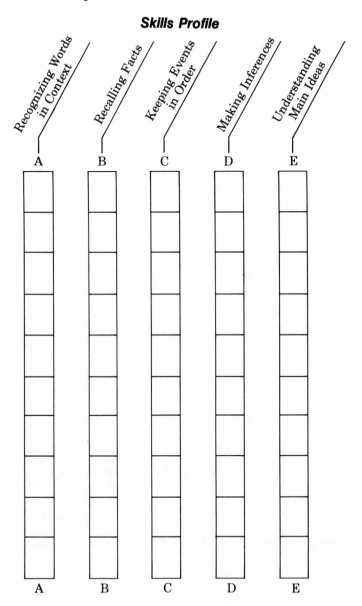